A hand-span up from the horizon, something dimly flickered. It was in the same vicinity as the Weggismarche Obelisk — it could, in fact, have been the top of the spire — and it suggested heat lightning on a warm summer night.

Suddenly, from across the sea, it was daylight. To the south the glow was dull gray and listless, but from the north the day was full and bright. Bar-Woten saw the Obelisk clearly, a line of white drawn from the sky down, its top lost in the sheet of daylight glow.

It was no longer vertical. With clocklike slowness it was changing its angle.... The Obelisk was tilting.... and falling.

Bar-Woten was enough of a seaman to know what the fall of an object a thousand kilometers high would do to the sea and to the coastline beyond....

GREG BEAR

Hegira

VGSF

VGSF is an imprint of Victor Gollancz Ltd
14 Henrietta Street, London WC2E 8QJ

First published in Great Britain 1987
by Victor Gollancz Ltd

First VGSF edition 1987

Original text copyright © 1979 by Greg Bear
Revised text copyright © 1987 by Greg Bear

British Library Cataloguing in Publication Data
Bear, Greg
  Hegira.
  I. Title
  813'.54[F]   PS3552.E157

ISBN 0-575-04008-4

Printed and bound in Great Britain
by Richard Clay (The Chaucer Press) Ltd, Bungay, Suffolk

This book is dedicated to Tina

"I had a dream, which was not all a dream.
The bright sun was extinguish'd, and the stars
Did wander darkling in the eternal space,
Rayless, and pathless, and the icy earth
Swung blind and blackening in the moonless air;
Morn came and went — and came, and brought
   no day . . ."

                    — *Darkness*, by Lord Byron

PEOPLE of the WALL

ENGLISH-SPEAKERS

PALE SEAS

WEGGISMARCHE

NIK

BICHT av
GENEVAR

PALLASTA

MAPPU
GOLUMBINE

AREA OF MAP

249,000 KM

OCEAN OBELISK

OBELISK
DIANA

MADREGHB

NIUR-ES-WERD

UBIDHARM

RIVER UB

MUNDUS
LUCIFA

OBELISKTARA

MEDIWEVA

TRINCOMA

OBELISK
ONMASSEE

FEDDERLAND

AREA CROSSED IN

HEGIRA

SCALE 1 cm ≅ 1000 KM

1978 G. BEAR

One

The short, stocky Ibisian general motioned for his aides to step up to the balcony. "Look closely," he told them as they stood next to the Mediwevan deputato. "Here's true barbarism."

Below the balcony, a parade of penitents filled the rain-slicked streets.

"These are ascetics from Monta Ignazio, General Sulay," the deputato stuttered. His teeth were chattering. He had never been closer to his country's savage, unwelcome guests than he was now.

The methane lanterns in the room hissed.

"They whip themselves," Bar-Woten said. He was a lean, well-muscled man in his middle thirties, with one gray eye and a black patch. His nose hooked sharply.

The penitents had gathered from leagues around for the night march through Mediweva's capital, Madreghb. Men, women, and children dressed in brown sacks, black and white clerical robes, or the red of deacons and priests swung leather cats against their backs, the strands weighted to age and devotion. Beneath cloth tatters their flesh was raw as ground meat.

"This is religious inspiration!" Sulay rasped. "The Heisos Kristos of Mediweva demands that they poison their bodies with infection to see His visions. Absorb this and learn from it. We've met with many peoples and their religions, but none is more amazing than this."

Bar-Woten watched with distaste and finally turned away. His eye caught the deputato's, and he winked at the thin official. "Not to my style," he explained. "I grow faint at the sight of blood." The deputato laughed nervously, then lapsed back to respectful silence.

Sulay stepped back from the balcony, shaking his head and fingering his pistol's holster strap. "I'd like to visit your library now." The deputato nodded and led him away. Bar-Woten stayed behind to watch the penitents flogging themselves. Their moans bothered him like a boil under his armored vest. They were ecstatic. The ecstasy of visions. "Barthel!" he called. His servant appeared, grinning and dressed in splendid red silks.

"I think I could like living here," Barthel said, fanning his arms out. "It's cool and the clothes are beautiful."

"What can you tell me about Kristians?"

"My country had a few, Bey. But I am of the Momad persuasion myself, as you understand, and we avoid inter-course with the unfaithful. Except for yourself, sir, who shine like the light . . . "

"'Shines,'" Bar-Woten corrected. "Your lessons in Mediwevan are slipping." He had chosen Barthel from a group of captured children fifteen years before in the now desolate land of Khem. The armies of Sulay, Bar-Woten among them, were responsible for that desolation. But Bar-thel showed no memory of the slaughter. He knew only those things he was required to know, and the rest seemed to sink in his memory like plum stones in a pond. He was a cheerful lad.

"Bey, I could tell you tales my mother told me, but some are very crazy. You might not believe. This Heisos Kristos — or Yesu as we knew him — is mentioned in all the Obelisks I have ever known, and his story is always the same."

"Which is food for the argument that all Obelisks have the same words engraved on them."

"Certainly. I believe that is part of Momad's divine doctrine, as his word is mentioned on all, the faithful must acknowledge that, and — "

"Why do they beat themselves for this Heisos?"

"It gives them strength to deny the attractions of the world, Bey. By punishing themselves they hope to distract their attentions from Hegira and focus them on Paradise, or Heaven, which is what their Yesu — surely a great prophet — desired and preached them to do."

"But Yesu never lived on Hegira."

"No. It is dogma that no person mentioned on the Obelisks ever lived on Hegira. They were the First-born, Bey."

Bar-Woten nodded and stared up into the night. Soon an orange fire dove would rise like a distant flare, signaling the ninth hour of dark, and the sky would begin to turn purple. In a half hour it would be morning blue. The streets would be empty of pedestrians as Mediwevan law had decreed for five hundred years. The wagons and steam vehicles would travel from the fields and lakefronts, and the capital would come alive with day-life: markets and buyers, bookdealers and street historians, all wholesome services for a fee. Bar-Woten enjoyed this city and its peculiarities. He even felt a mixed affection for the crazy penitents.

"I can tell you very little about Yesu, Bey," Barthel said to indicate he had not been dismissed. Bar-Woten waved his hand, and the boy vanished with a rustle of robes.

He was glad not enough of Sulay's armies was left to destroy Mediweva. In their twenty-year March the armies had dwindled from two million to ten thousand. They could still rely on their reputation to achieve diplomatic victories, and on occasion a few hills topped by lines of the remaining

11

soldiers could persuade reluctant leaders, but the March was over.

They had crossed fifty thousand kilometers, the regions of five Obelisks, and yet spanned only twenty-three degrees of Hegira's curve. The survivors of Sulay's March knew the immensity of Hegira as no others had known before them. For two years now, since the last of their geographers and geometers had finished their reports, Bar-Woten had marched in fear not of man — he had killed at least two thousand men, and they did not haunt him — but of the world on which he lived.

That evening Sulay called Bar-Woten to the library. The Ibisian left Barthel in their quarters and walked down the cool stone hallways of the capital palace, looking up at the frescoes crumbling in the dimly lit vaults. The sense of age oppressed him tonight. So many years, so much time to do evil things . . . layers and layers of human pressure bearing down on him like miles of rock.

The frescoes showed scenes of war taken from Obelisk texts. Bar-Woten felt the painter's lack of firsthand experience acutely, both proud and revolted by his own knowledge. Shaking his head and grimacing, he entered the door to the library.

The musty smell of paper and ink and old leather bindings hung heavy in the still air. The oxygen seemed to have been sucked out by years of rotting pulp. He restrained an impulse to choke. A middle-aged, balding librarian guided him through long, winding stacks and stopped, pointing with a knobby ink-stained finger calloused on the first knuckle.

Sulay sat on a stool, a large book spread across his lap. His gray hair and bald spot shone in the tier of oil lamps set beside him. Bar-Woten noted the pump-action fire extinguisher hung on a fixture.

"Young Bear-killer," Sulay said, looking up. Bar-Woten bowed slightly.

"The general needs his rest," he said solicitously.

Sulay ignored him. "The Mediwevans have ascended a little higher than we have," he said, thumbing the pages. "Better balloons, I imagine. More texts, more advances, but they haven't seen fit to apply their new knowledge, not yet. Many odd things as the texts go higher." Sulay closed the book carefully and placed it on a small folding table. "I could spend my whole life in libraries. Much less exciting than the March, eh?"

Bar-Woten nodded. Sulay's demeanor changed considerably when he was among books. Bar-Woten wasn't sure he approved, though something in himself was attracted to the endless shelves. "Less strenuous at least," he said.

"These people know us as soldiers, murderers, plunderers," Sulay said. "No doubt we've done enough of that. But they will never appreciate us as scholars. Yet what we could tell them! They know very little of Hegira, but a great deal of the Obelisks. I know very little of the Obelisks . . . and I wish I knew more. But . . . " He sighed. "My time is at an end, Bear-killer."

Bar-Woten respected the old man's lengthy silence. At last Sulay lifted his head, and there were tears on his cheeks. "Never enough time. Never enough. The March is over. They aren't very good at fighting here in Mediweva, but they far outnumber us, and our ruses aren't working any more. My audiences with the Holy Pontiff have been more and more strained. An old soldier's instincts warn me. . . . He will swat us like a buzzing wasp. Our reputation travels before us, even in the insular countries. We have not been circumspect." Sulay looked Bar-Woten steadily in the eye. The old general's pupils were large, absorbing. "You will go on."

"Not without you, General."

"Without me, without your fellow soldiers, however you must. You'll finish the March. We didn't journey to kill and loot, but try telling that to an army of Ibisians . . . " Sulay put his hand on the book. "That's my commission to you. If anyone will survive, you will. Go now, or very soon."

Bar-Woten nodded.

"Go and find what I wanted to find."

"Yes, General."

"You would do that even if I didn't tell you, wouldn't you?"

"Yes."

Sulay picked up the book again and opened it.

"It isn't safe here, General," Bar-Woten said. "They can come from both directions and pen you in."

Sulay didn't react.

"General?"

The old man dismissed Bar-Woten with a gesture. He turned and walked through the stacks, fists clenched.

The morning of their ninth day in Madreghb brought clouded skies and a pale drizzle that turned the capital into a fairy-tale province. The richly carved walls of the Duomo and the Middle Sacristy attracted Bar-Woten and dazzled Barthel as they walked alone through the city. Wearing his dress whites and a windbreaker, and according Barthel the same privilege, he ignored the damp and studied the architecture.

The courtyard of learned debate drew him as sugar draws an ant. Here scholars, readers, and Obelisk students gathered with their practical counterparts — engineers, geometers, and theologicians. They debated loudly over a narrow road-way separating their bleachers, below an aqueduct carrying water from the southern branch of the Ub. Cars and trucks hissed between them irregularly. The white drizzle beaded and dripped from the debaters' black leather cloaks, pooling on the wooden planks that ran the length of the stone seats.

Barthel was amused. "They discuss the teachings of Yesu," he whispered in an aside to Bar-Woten. He nodded and listened more closely. They stood on a walkway bridge mounted on one side of the aqueduct. Water rushed to its appointments behind them, splattered with occasional raindrops.

One theologician kept his dignity and calm amidst the ruckus. He commanded a fine voice and his wit was incisive. They listened for a while, then moved on. Bar-Woten frowned as they left the aqueduct. Had Heisos, or Yesu, been a firm warrior with words or a debater of pedantries?

The weather worsened. Lunching in a smoky wooden parlor-house with glass windows slacked by age, they watched the drizzle thicken into rain, much as the grease of a lamb congealed on their plates. "I change my mind about the cold; it is unpleasant," Barthel said, drawing his jacket collar tight around his ears. "I often wish the Bey had chosen to reside in Khem, where it is usually warm." Bar-Woten nodded.

The day would soon collapse into dark. He didn't enjoy the thought of walking after dark to the capital square and the Nocturne, essentially unarmed. It was unhealthy.

They set out just before the dimming began. At this season the days were ten hours long and the nights fourteen. The weather promised to be foul in the dark. The wind nipped and curled around their backs, making their eyes sting. Cats scampered in a wet tide from one alley into another, yowling miserably. Bar-Woten saw why as they passed the alley — a rain gutter edging the roof of the inn had broken, turning a dry corner into the base of a cascade.

"It would be good to take shelter," Barthel said from under his jacket. The boy's eyebrows, bushy at the best of times, now knitted to form a solid ragged streak across his brow. His dark brown eyes were slitted against the raindrops.

Bar-Woten shielded his good eye and looked at the entrance to the hostel. He knew instinctively it would be a vermin paradise. But he distrusted wet weather in strange countries. Enough diseases had plagued him in similar conditions to make him wary.

"Wait," Barthel said, peering back into the alley where the cats had lodged. The cascade had subsided to a trickle. Something moved at the back. It was shapeless, larger than a man. Barthel stepped backward and Bar-Woten's neck hair rose.

He wiped his eye with the knuckle of his thumb. The shape was nothing monstrous after all. A man was struggling under a pile of wet papers and rags, weak and unpromising labor at best. The Ibisian's first thought was to leave well enough alone — this possible plague victim was no friend to a visitor without immunity. But the man was not sick with plague; he was weak from blood loss. They approached him cautiously. Bar-Woten crouched next to the pile.

The man was a penitent. His whip was still hooked to his belt, lashes tangled in his scraped and bruised legs. But this young fellow was no priest or professional ascetic. He was barely twenty and nearly dead. His back wounds had festered enough to give him fever visions sufficient for a lifetime. Now he was unconscious. Bar-Woten called for Barthel to help and together they picked him up by the arms and legs. "We'll take him to the hostel," he said.

"He's in bad shape," Barthel said. "He'll die soon anyway."

The hostel desk was unstaffed. The interior of the building was fitfully lighted by gas lamps. Disintegrating wallpaper crept up the walls, and the floor creaked suspiciously. A smell of wet, decaying wood mixed with the animal smell of the hostel's patrons. It was a miserable place for anyone to die in. Therefore, Bar-Woten told himself, the young man would not die.

He rang a verdigris-crusted bell. The half-sotted proprietor appeared shortly after. He took their names and their money and raised a hairless, worm-white eyebrow at the penitent. "Can you get a physician?" Bar-Woten asked.

"No," the proprietor said, heading back to his room. "If he dies, you'll have to move him."

"I am an Ibisian," Bar-Woten said softly. "If this man dies here, I will have this building condemned."

The proprietor stopped and turned to reexamine him. "You can find a doctor a block down. We have nothing to do with penitents. They aren't too popular here."

"And Ibisians?" Bar-Woten asked testily.

"Unarmed Ibisians are only human," the proprietor said. "I employ bullboys like every other innkeeper on this strip. They carry rifles and crossguns. Do you?" He turned and waddled off.

Bar-Woten picked up the key from the desk and told Barthel to summon the physician. He hoisted the penitent from the floor and swung him over his shoulder.

The stairs were steep and in bad repair. The room was abominable. An open skylight admitted rain until he tied a dirty blanket over it. The beds were in fair repair and looked clean. Perhaps health regulations were enforced with regard to beds, but cleaning facilities were minimal, toilets were one to a floor and public, and other regulations ended at the edge of the mattress. Paper scraps and dirt littered the torn patchwork carpet.

The penitent sighed and rolled over on the bed, then groaned. Bar-Woten stripped off his bloody clothes and took the basin down the hall to clean it and fill it with water. The plumbing banged hideously in the narrow washroom. When

17

he came back the man was sitting up against the headboard and staring feverishly into empty space. Using a handful of powdered soap and paper towels, Bar-Woten began to scrub him down. Few of the wounds were deeply infected. Nevertheless, he knew an antiseptic and clean bandages would have to be applied, or blood poisoning would set in. He had seen small wounds fester into deadly foul pockets many times on the March.

Barthel returned with a small, seam-faced doctor a half hour later. The man said his name was Luigi, examined the penitent quickly, and expressed his reluctance to treat him. "He's one of God's own," he said. "God will take care of him."

"You will take care of him, or he'll die," said Bar-Woten. "You wouldn't want to be charged with malpractice, would you? I can take you before a deputato if you wish."

The little doctor shrugged and set his bag down. "You cleaned him?" he asked. Bar-Woten nodded. "I'll have to do it over again," the doctor complained. "He's whipped himself into a fine fever."

An hour later the penitent was bandaged and sleeping fitfully. "He'll be weak for a day, maybe longer. Why do you want to help a penitent? Did he ask for help?"

Bar-Woten didn't answer. Barthel thanked the doctor and paid him a gold piece. They sat in silence and fell asleep before morning.

Bar-Woten stood by the skylight on a rickety stool, lifting the stained blanket and peering out across the smoke-tracked foggy rooftops at the wan morning light. The slate and tile roofs glistened with an oily sheen of dew and reflected the golden zenith. The horizon was still deep blue. The zenith light expanded and turned yellowish, then green. In a wink the green accomplished its magical transformation into blue. A steam cart hissed and rattled in an alley below.

"Won't the master Sulay miss us, Bey?" Barthel asked sleepily from his blanket on the floor.

"Not for a while," Bar-Woten answered. He turned to look at the man on the bed. His breathing was light and regular. His pale face had taken on a better color during the night. He looked almost healthy.

Bar-Woten checked his pulse and pinched his fingernails, and still the man slept. Barthel said pounding rocks together wouldn't wake a healing man before his body was ready.

"You told me your mother knew stories about Kristians," Bar-Woten said. "Do you remember any of them?"

For the briefest of moments the boy's face clouded and his eyes narrowed. Then it was clear again and he smiled. "Not too well, Bey. Mostly derogatory stories about their customs, which I am no longer qualified to criticize since I share them with you very often. The eating of unclean foods, the drinking of wine and other forbidden beverages."

"Nothing about why a man would drive himself to illness to meet his god?"

"No, Bey."

It was perhaps the same reason two million men had once left the beautiful land of Ibis to cross the Atlasade range into Barthel's land, Khem. Or why they had tortured themselves by crossing the Pais Vermagne, a thousand kilometers of swamp and pestilence and deadly reptiles, instead of taking an easier route — all to investigate legends in Khem of the City of the First-born. They had found a monotonous grassland and a central range of hills as barren and dusty as the deserts west of Ibis. No treasure, no fabled city.

The penitent was also searching for treasure, and his trek was just as rugged. Bar-Woten questioned his own sanity in feeling sympathy, but he did. Sympathy and warmth. *Welcome, fellow traveler. How many souls have you killed inside*

*yourself trying to find the right one to present to God, saying,
Look — pure!*

Surely not as many souls as I have killed, he thought, *mostly
in the bodies of others.*

"Hello," the penitent said. Bar-Woten started from his
reverie and looked at the man sternly. The pale face returned
the stare like a statue. The lips were fever-cracked, the
nostrils red with broken vessels. "You've put me up for the
night?"

"Nothing honorable," Bar-Woten said. "You nearly killed
yourself. Most people's gods resent suicide."

"Where am I?"

"A hostel."

"I have to leave." The penitent's watery green eyes filled
with enormous black pupils. The corners of his mouth
turned up perpetually, and his eyes crinkled at their edges as
though, like a mischievous child, he might laugh at any
moment. But these were betrayals of his body. He was
perfectly serious.

"Nobody's holding you. You should get your strength
back, however. Eat some food."

"I'm on a fast."

"For how long? Until you starve?"

"I'm starving now. It brings me closer to my goal."

"And what is your goal?"

"To live in the light of God, not the mud of the world."

"What's your name?"

"Jacome. Yours?"

"Bar-Woten."

"A peculiar name."

"I'm an Ibisian. I picked the name up when I killed a bear
fifteen years ago. He clawed out an eye before he died. Bear-
killer, of the One-eyed God. Bar-Woten. Why do you call
yourself Jacome? That's not your name. Am I right that

penitents, if they try to deny the world, must deny themselves? Change their names?"

"Yes," Jacome said. "Fools of God. Buffoons."

"Then what was your name before you changed?"

"You'd have to ask the fellow I was. I can't answer."

Bar-Woten motioned for Barthel to leave.

"Tell me about your god," he said.

"You're interested?"

"I am."

Barthel sat outside and leaned against the wall. His eyes surveyed the ceiling, searching for bugs to amuse him, certainly not interested by the drivel being spoken inside. He did not understand his master at times. It was often hard to like Bar-Woten. He was kind, but he loved nothing. Barthel, on the other hand, wished to love everything. That was impossible with Bar-Woten constantly calling for him. The man's gloom was sometimes appalling.

Bar-Woten interrupted Jacome's discourse long enough to debate a few points of logic. "This Heisos, also known as Yesu, is on every Obelisk across Hegira, right?"

"He is."

"Then why isn't everyone converted by His truth?"

"Because there are words on the Obelisks that contradict what He taught. Inspired by the adversary."

"How do you know which to choose, which is right?"

"By the heart, the way it beats to the right words."

"Did Heisos live on Hegira?"

"No."

"Then was His mission intended for the Second-born?"

"For all humanity."

Barthel paced in the hallway, bent to listen at the door, then had an inspiration. He would go out for food. But he had very little of the Bey's money with him. He knocked cautiously. No answer. They were still talking. He feared the penitent might convert the Bey. A dreadful thing. He knocked again. Bar-Woten opened the door.

"Master, shall I buy food for all of us?"

The Bey looked at him intensely through his single eye, then reached into his jacket pocket for a coin. "Good food, fresh, and a variety of it. Enough to last all of us for a day or so."

Barthel grinned and ran off.

Bar-Woten shut the door and asked Jacome another question. "What made you find the grace of Kristos?"

"The guidance of my heart."

"Can you remember what made you follow your heart?"

Jacome scowled. "It's only important that I found the truth in time."

"But you forget what happened. Was it someone who helped you?"

"I haven't forgotten. No one helped me at first. But when I joined the Franciscans, they helped me."

"I want to know what converted you. Perhaps I can find something like it in myself."

Barthel found his idea less attractive when he stood on the street. There were no food stalls nearby. The Bey's presence, at any rate, was always reassuring. Now, alone in a city he did not know well, he felt his pulse rise and his eyes widen. The people did not look harmful. Still, any city held thieves, cutthroats, pickpockets. Monsters to suck a poor Momadan dry. The Bey's teachings from Barthel's youth could not eradicate this fear.

As Barthel walked, swaggering slightly and looking from side to side to show his confidence, he thought of the comforts of Khem and how they had passed in such an inconceivably short time. The Bey had never bothered to explain or excuse the actions of Sulay in Khem — and for this Barthel was thankful. He didn't think he could stand

the propaganda other servants told him they were regaled with. Bar-Woten was a good master.

But if it ever came to light who had killed his father and mother and two sisters . . . Barthel's swagger stiffened. He didn't know what he would do. He was young and no fighter. At times he wished he could be a fighter and kill Sulay, cold fishy Sulay, who cared only for kilometers crossed and confirmations of the greatness of Sulay.

But food was the order of the moment. He found a clean-looking stall that purveyed crullers, tins of coffee, and fresh vegetables. He didn't bother with the meat. Ibisians, like Momadans on Hegira, were not meat-eaters for the most part. They preferred vegetables, fruits, and fish or fowl.

He bargained rapidly and without mercy. The stall's owner, a man four times Barthel's age, smiled and gave in a little. Eventually a price was reached and they hooked thumbs, Mediwevan style.

The parcels were heavy. Barthel decided to rent a cart. He hailed a bicycle-drawn taxi when he saw no carts were available. The hack was little older than himself and regarded him with sharp dark eyes and taut lips. The fare hardly seemed worth pulling. But the hack mounted his wooden bike and pedaled without strain up and down the flat-cobbled dips and gutters. Barthel relaxed his guard to look at the surroundings more leisurely. It didn't seem a bad city. Busy people were everywhere, and few were lame or crippled or ill-looking.

The Bey was still talking with the penitent when Barthel returned. The young man was sweating and looked upset. His hand motions were jagged, and he stammered. The Bey was as firm and persistent as ever. Barthel dropped the packages in a corner and sat down to listen.

"I can't tell you how I saw the wisdom of the Lord Heisos. It's a private matter."

"Can there be private matters between two souls striving for salvation?"

"For this soul there is. You may confess what you wish."

"Fra Jacome, I have learned much from you. Would you care to raise your health for God's work by joining us in breaking fast?"

"You sound pious, Fra Bar-Woten. I know you're not. You're ridiculing me.'

"I am sincere. I wish you to join us in our meal."

"You know I can't eat until the Fast of Francis is over."

Barthel disapproved of what the Bey was doing. He was baiting the penitent, drawing him onto limbs and cutting them out from under. The Bey had a deadly way of finding out how other people thought, like dissection. Barthel allowed himself a moment of judgment on his master.

"Your health will break and you'll die."

"Why are you interested in my health? Your people would sooner destroy us than spit on us!"

Bar-Woten shrugged and lifted his eyebrow. "I can't speak for other Ibisians. Perhaps they do. Me, I wish to know what makes a man whip himself in the name of a God Who is kind."

"My God is not kind!" Jacome bellowed. "He takes away cruelly and has no mercy for those who do not know and perform His wishes!"

Barthel cringed in surprise. The Bey had found the weak point he wanted.

"Then how did you come to love Him? Out of fear?"

The penitent tried to speak, but stammered into silence. His eyes were bright with tears and anger. "You p-p-pry," he managed to stutter. "You t-twist my tongue like a serpent."

"I am curious," Bar-Woten said. "And concerned."

"I saw the light of God in the middle of an agony so great

24

I couldn't stand it. I grieved so deeply I died. And when I was reborn, I was the child you see now, still not mature in God's eyes. I was a scrittori. I recorded the writings on the Obelisk. I was going to marry a woman of my own age in a village near Obelisk Tara. We were nine months betrothed." He paused and caught his breath, his wild look abating.

"She had been born the same day as a boy in Castoreto. They came from different families, but they looked alike. Some said they were twins by God's will. This boy was an apprentice scrittori. I knew him from our schooling. He fell from the side of the Obelisk and died, and that same day my only life and love froze hard as a block of ice. Her skin became a mirror. Nothing could revive her. That is what killed me — a touch from God's finger told me not to adore the beauties of the world!"

It was Bar-Woten's turn to be astonished. Speechless, he stepped away from the bed and walked to the skylight. "Doppelgangers, I think," he mused softly. Barthel cocked his head. "Do you remember the story?" the Bey asked him.

Barthel nodded, a little shiver going up his back.

Two

Jacome sat in bed with his face frozen, staring stonily at the opposite wall. One finger tapped on the counterpane. He seemed willing to sit that way forever.

Bar-Woten ate a quick breakfast. Barthel joined him on the floor, eating ravenously. His master kept no eye on the penitent, so Barthel observed him closely.

"What does it mean to you?" Jacome finally asked.

"It's an old story," Bar-Woten answered around a bite of melon. "A fable. The Princess and the Poor Man."

"It's no story. It happened."

"I don't doubt that," Bar-Woten said, turning around on his hindquarters to face the bed. "What was your name then?"

"Kiril."

"And you felt God was punishing you."

"She was all I loved."

"It's ridiculous to believe God would punish someone else for your own wrongdoings. That's ego, not Kristianity."

"I know that." Jacome-Kiril flushed like an embarrassed child. "Why did you pull me out of hiding?"

"I don't know," Bar-Woten said.

"I can't go back."

"You've never heard the story of the Princess and the Poor Man?"

"No. I never enjoyed children's stories."

"I doubt it even exists in Mediweva, or someone would

have pointed it out to you long ago. It's about a Poor Man who wins a contest for the heart of a great king's daughter. The day before their wedding she's transformed into a silver statue as hard as diamond. The king searches the land for the responsible sorcerer, but never finds him. However, he learns a peasant family had a son born the same day as his daughter. They resembled each other so much they could have been twins. The boy had died at the moment of his daughter's affliction. The Poor Man was stricken with grief."

"I don't believe you."

"You might find the end interesting. A seeress tells the Poor Man who won the contest that he must travel very far to save his bride-to-be — to the Land Where Night Is a River. He will find the Princess's male doppelganger, or double, when he crosses over that empty river to the land beyond. When he returns the double to the king's land, the Princess will be restored. He does as he is told, and she comes back to life."

Kiril stared at Bar-Woten. The pain in his expression was too much for Barthel. He turned his eyes away.

"First you pull me out of my cave, and now you tell me there's some way to bring back my most precious love."

"How could I have known about your grief?" Bar-Woten asked. "I'm no monster. Ask any Ibisian. It's a story known to all of us."

"God damn you!" Kiril spat.

Bar-Woten faced the penitent with a stare as implacable as his own. He smiled. "Barthel," he said without turning, "prepare our belongings and wrap up the rest of the food. We're leaving." Then, his smile gone, he said, "Perhaps it's an offer, a chance to regain what you've lost."

"How? By some fantasy?"

"That, or let your body and mind rot in a life you're not suited for. Come with us."

"You want me to travel with your army?"

"There is no army," the Ibisian said coldly. "Soon there will be no Sulay. The dirt will absorb us like the end of a river. I owe no allegiance to a dead dream. I've been looking for a reason to go. I now have a reason."

Barthel was genuinely frightened. The Bey talked nonsense, believing a mad Kristian and thinking a fairy-tale coincidence could point like a beacon! Momad save them all.

"We're both insane," Kiril said softly. "I pity you more than myself."

"Pity no one. There's no room for it. I have other reasons to make a journey. Some mysteries to solve."

"What can possibly mystify a madman?"

"The world. The origin of the flesh. But mostly the world, our world. Why we are Second-born and take our truths from Obelisks." He sighed and saw that Barthel had finished packing the food and their meager burden of clothes. "Are you well enough to travel?"

"I can walk. You compel me to follow?"

"As one madman to another. I pulled you out of one cave, now I'm obligated to watch over you."

"It wasn't much of a cave," Kiril admitted. "I haven't met your companion."

"This is Barthel, from Khem." Barthel bowed and almost dropped the sack from his shoulder. "But he won't be my servant for long. I won't force anyone to follow me."

"Where does the Bey think he will go?" Barthel asked.

"To the Land Where Night Is a River," he answered. "Or at the very least, to my death."

Three

"I don't think we're welcome here, Bey," Barthel said. The horse market was crowding with scowling onlookers.

Kiril swept his tattered robes over his shoulder and tightened the rope that held them together. "Something's in the wind."

"We'll stay close together," Bar-Woten said. "I think this trader wants our money more than our necks. I'll bargain. You two keep close watch." He returned to haggling with the rheumy-eyed horse dealer. The man puffed his cheeks out at Bar-Woten's offer and held up his hands. "Too cheap," he said. "These mounts are noble beasts worth twice that at least. Let's say four fifty apiece."

"Robbery," Bar-Woten said calmly. "Two fifty is all we have for horses today. We will buy elsewhere."

"Three seventy-five," the dealer said, not batting an eye.

"Too much." Bar-Woten turned and motioned for his companions to follow. The dealer ran after them, looking concerned, but a small, portly man waddled from a nearby stall and whispered in his ear. The dealer stopped and raised his bushy gray eyebrows.

"Not too high a price for a hunted man," he said loudly.

Bar-Woten twisted around and threw a needle stare at the trader. The man squirmed like a pinned insect, then started to back off. The crowd moved in a step at a time, grumbling and milling about.

"Knife," Bar-Woten said. Barthel quickly passed a blade

under cover of their cloaks. He pressed another into Kiril's hand. "If we don't have a chance, save your skin. But go on your own," the Ibisian said. "It's your only chance, penitent."

"Is that too high a price for an Ibisian?" the trader asked contemptuously. "For a butcher?"

"For any sensible man," Bar-Woten answered, approaching him with a long stride. "Perhaps you'll lower your price with some persuasion?" The trader backed away farther. He looked at the market crowd with darting eyes and held out his hands to them — attack, now! But they did nothing, still advancing slowly.

"Hup!" Bar-Woten shouted. Barthel rushed forward and pushed the trader aside. Kiril followed at his heels. The crowd leaped as one and Bar-Woten swung his curved knife wickedly this way and that, making them flex like a sheet in the wind. Then he ran backward with comic agility, turned at the last moment, and swung onto a horse Barthel had secured for him. Kiril, unaccustomed to his own mount, had trouble controlling the animal's bucking and rearing, but was keeping the mob back. Barthel reached for the Mediwevan's reins and pulled him after as Bar-Woten cut a path through the market. The crowd screamed and grabbed at ankles, stirrups, whatever they could reach. For their efforts they were kicked and cuffed and thrust aside by the running horses. The three broke from the marketplace and rode up an alley, stopping briefly to reconnoiter.

"Which way?" Kiril asked, out of breath and red-faced with exertion.

"The east gate to the left. Farmlands and a road to the forests. The best way," Bar-Woten said. He urged his horse forward and the others followed. Behind them the market crowd surged up the alley.

There were no troops between them and the gate. In the

30

misty morning light, bright and uniformly gray, they rode up the cobbled streets with forced equanimity. The horses pitched their heads and frothed at the bits, unaccustomed to their new riders and uncertain of the adventure.

Barthel's animal laid its ears back and tried to bite him several times. On the last attempt, just before they passed under the great stone arch, Barthel leaned forward and took an ear between his teeth. The animal bucked and kicked out, narrowly missing an old woman wobbling by in her black robes. But Barthel held on, and the horse decided to be calm.

"Farewell to Madreghb," Bar-Woten said as they rode under the gate. Kiril looked uncomfortable. Barthel surveyed the green country beyond with dark-eyed nonchalance.

"Does the Bey know where he wants to go?" he asked.

"North. We'll cross the border into Mundus Lucifa as soon as we can. Sulay's met his end, and ours will be close behind if we don't move quickly."

"Your army generated a lot of good will," Kiril said.

"Keep on your horse and watch your mouth when you're an outlaw. Honor among thieves is a virtue seldom observed — be glad I'm not often a thief and no longer an Ibisian."

"And I no longer have God on my side."

"Your journey is a noble one, penitent. You're off to save your love. We ride hard for an hour or so — hang on!"

The land outside the scattered and crumbling walls of Madreghb was fresh and fertile with spring rains. Almond trees blossomed yellow in groves on either side, and olive orchards hunkered gray-green in aging shadow. The road was a reddish-brown gash infrequently paved with flagstones and littered with ruts and puddles. Their horses splashed through at a dead run. The flanks of both mounts and riders were soon sticky with mud. Kiril bounced and growled at

31

growing blisters. "Ride loosely, ride with the horse," Bar-Woten shouted at him, but he continued to wrap his feet under the horse's belly and soon had welts on his calves, thighs, and buttocks.

He sighed aloud when they stopped at a tumbledown farmhouse to examine a well. "My God, adventure!" Kiril rasped. "I might ask to die after another hour of that." His vision swam and he wanted to vomit.

"You'll get used to it," Barthel told him.

"You were whipping yourself only three days ago," Bar-Woten reminded him. "Which punishment do you prefer?"

The well was full, but the water was brackish. Still, it was drinkable, and they watered their horses, watching carefully that they didn't bloat themselves. Bar-Woten inspected his horse. It was a dapple roan, very different from any he'd ridden in his army. He made sure the shoeing was holding up. The smithy work was rugged and durable, and no stones had worked into the hooves. He did the same for the other mounts and pronounced them fit. "Ready?" he asked.

This time they rode at an even pace. The smell of damp leather and warm horse rose to cheer Bar-Woten and made Barthel feel at home, but Kiril wrinkled his nose. By midafternoon, the Mediwevan was weary but only a little nauseated. His back was still slightly infected. They found a stand of oaks and settled in for a prolonged rest.

Across the valley, no more than three or four kilometers away, a village rested in the late afternoon twilight. The white walls and red brick roads stood out in the dimming golden light like the bones and meat of a freshly-slaughtered steer. Bar-Woten watched it with narrowed eyes. Barthel napped, and Kiril lay on his stomach in the grass and loam, breathing fitfully.

He struggled awake an hour later and stretched painfully, pulling at the lash stripes across his shoulders. "I wish I hadn't been so thorough," he said. Bar-Woten smoked beside the small fire. Darkness was complete. The Ibisian's face glowed in the firelight, and the reflection of the pipe coals was a bead of red on his nose. "I wish I knew what I was doing here," Kiril said, "with a savage like yourself and a pagan."

"You gave up one life," Bar-Woten mused. "Not so difficult to give up another, especially one with no rewards."

"I'm a coward, I think," Kiril said. "I haven't had the conviction to stay with any sort of life."

Bar-Woten gave a noncommittal nod and put out his pipe, pointing the stem at the village after grinding the ashes into the ground. "We'll pick up supplies there. We have a long trip ahead — several hundred kilometers, maybe, before we leave Mediweva."

"Less than that," Kiril said. "What happened in Madreghb? You have any idea?"

"Sulay probably let his guard down. He was getting too old to be vigilant all the time. No doubt he was the last to die, though I think I see him . . . how he died. Not bravely. The way we led our lives, few of us will die bravely now."

"You . . . think of yourself as a savage?"

"Of course," Bar-Woten said. "Twenty years of March and battle. How could I be anything but a savage? I haven't married a fine woman or fathered good children, and my religion departed years ago at my own hand. I've killed men brutally. And you're an ass to travel with me." He grinned.

"Probably," Kiril admitted.

Barthel woke quickly and doused the embers with urine. They gathered the horses at their tethers near a small, grassy glade and rode into the village under cover of darkness.

"Did you enjoy being a scrittori?" Bar-Woten asked. Kiril nodded and said it had been the finest time of his life.

"Did you ever wish to verify what you read?"

"No. What's written on the Obelisk is taken for truth. Why else would God have gone to so much trouble?"

"Sh," Barthel hushed. A group of men leading donkeys passed them on the road, briefly flashing a lantern. No words passed between.

Most of the village was shuttered and quiet for the night. A few shops were open still, but the hungry and sleepy owners were grumpy at any customers. They bought food and two small pistols.

Bar-Woten decided it wasn't wise to spend the night in the village. He could almost smell the pursuers.

"When people want you dead, you always assume the worst," he said. Kiril drew his horse closer to the center of the road as they left the town. Barthel stopped, and his mount pawed the ground impatiently. Bar-Woten turned to the Khemite and also reined in his horse. In the dark, with only a few dim fire doves to light the landscape, he could barely see the road, and he couldn't tell what Barthel was thinking.

"Does the Bey wish me to follow, or does he wish me to go alone?"

"You are free to choose."

"I'm not used to that."

"You're free to come with us if you want."

"I'm no longer your servant?"

"You haven't been for a day or so, maybe longer."

"I would like to go with you then."

"Good."

Barthel brought his horse up even with theirs, and they marched abreast in the dark.

Bar-Woten was the next to call a halt. He perked his head up and listened intently. "Engines," he said. Kiril could hear nothing but insects humming. Barthel kept silent, knowing Bar-Woten's senses were sharper than his own.

"They're about a kilometer back, near the village. Steam buggies. And I think horses, too. We'll have to ride hard to reach the next hills before them." He spurred his horse, and the group galloped off. Kiril groaned aloud with each lurch. They reached the hills and heard the clear hiss-chug of a steam buggy just as lights appeared on the road behind them. Shadows of horses prancing across the light-beams gave Bar-Woten a rough idea how many were following them. It was a large group, maybe twenty men. He looked around desperately and saw a ravine angling away from the road, not too deep to climb out of, but deep enough to hide them if the horses could be kept quiet. It pointed to a dense copse of trees where they'd have a better chance in a fight.

"Your horse," he called back to Kiril. "To keep it quiet, pull both its ears back gently and tug with every sound it makes — but not too hard!" They left the road and slid into the ravine one by one, rocks and clods rattling behind. The soft sandy bottom muffled the pounding hooves. Water splashed and clouds of insects rose to feather them and cling.

Trees grew above the ravine after a hundred meters of winding run. Bar-Woten found the way ahead blocked, brought his horse up short, and urged it to clamber up the side of the ravine into the copse. It hesitated and reeled but finally dug its hooves into the soft dirt and hauled itself up the slope. Barthel and Kiril followed. A bag of supplies dropped from Kiril's horse, and he turned instinctively to retrieve it. "No!" Barthel stage-whispered. "Leave it!"

Already the chugging and clop of hooves was clearly audible. The pursuers were no more than a hundred meters from where the ravine began. The buggy wouldn't be able to follow, but the horses could give them a dangerous chase.

Branches whipped by as they plunged through the trees. Bar-Woten held up his hand to push them aside and gritted his teeth at the sting. A stem slapped Kiril across the mouth, and he felt blood on his lips, but he didn't dare stop. "This is mad," he whispered to himself, licking his lips.

Barthel's horse seemed to lose its footing. It teetered, whinnied sharply, and vanished like a ghost. Kiril shouted for Bar-Woten to stop and pulled his horse around to go back. "Hey!" he called in a harsh whisper. "Hey! What's happened?"

He couldn't see anything. The fire doves were nearly down now. It would be a few minutes before other bright ones rose to replace them. He heard the shouts of approaching men and the distant chatter and rumble of the idling steam buggy. But Barthel was not to be seen or heard. Kiril cursed Bar-Woten. He ground his teeth and slapped his horse's flank in frustration. The animal jumped, then stood its ground shivering and champing on its bit. "He's ridden away, damn him!"

The forest was now completely dark. Lanterns gleamed from the road, and some bobbed closer, carried by men on horseback. A bright spot came on at the back of the steam buggy, and a whining generator matched the chug, chug, hiss. The light scoured the forest, formed a blinding band on a tree over Kiril's head, passed by, then circled back on the ground. He moved his horse to one side. The upper arc of the circle passed within inches of the horse's hooves. He didn't dare speak or call out names, so he guided his horse between two oaks and dismounted. Should he grab the animal's ears to keep it quiet? He decided not to. He patted its neck and whispered to it, not audible above the wind in the trees. He held his hand up and moved his fingers to see what he could detect — nothing. The pitchy woods were full of odd sounds now that he was blind — sighs of tree limbs, leaves rustling, water groaning over rocks someplace near.

He couldn't see the lanterns from behind the tree, but he could see their backwash. He heard the voices plainly.

36

"Tracks! Dirt gouged up here."

"Yes, but which way? Did they double back?"

"How many are there?"

"Too many! Damned Ibisians would sooner cut a throat than eat dinner."

"Many would say one leads to the other."

"Quiet! What's that?"

Kiril listened and tried to stop his own breathing. His horse was cooperating and he felt a great affection for it. Wonderful beast!

"Nothing. Leaves."

"Don't be too sure, dammit."

"Where's Reynot?"

"He was behind me."

"Reynot, Reynot!"

"Quiet!"

The lamps came into Kiril's line of sight, and he ducked closer to the trunk. There was nothing he could do about the horse. He could see their beams dodging back and forth steadily. One lamp fell and winked out. It didn't reappear. There was little sound now but the nickering of the animals.

"Where is Hispan?" The voice creaked with fear. Somewhere a bird twittered. Again the searchlight passed through the woods. It swept over someone hugging a tree like a lizard.

Who? Kiril couldn't tell. He began to tremble uncontrollably, and sweat stung his eyes. His teeth chattered and he bit his thumb to quiet them.

"We're losing ourselves here. Back off — is that a horse?"

Kiril jumped.

"It's Reynot's horse. Somebody got him!"

"Get together in a circle until the next fire dove rises. Quickly!"

"Hispan is gone. What's that?"

"Where?"

Kiril decided the best thing would be to leave. But which way? Away from the road he might run into what had swallowed Barthel. He had no judgment for distances at all. But he decided leading his horse out would be better than waiting for the next light. He tugged at the reins and urged the animal to follow. "Not a sound!" his lips said.

His feet felt their way in the dark with tiny crunches. His back prickled — at any moment he expected a light and a bullet. But they were still talking among themselves, about twenty meters back. A dim twinkle was starting to the north — another fire dove was rising, a bright one.

"Quiet — and step this way!" he heard Barthel say. "To your left."

They were waiting for him behind a thrust of granite. Bar-Woten had a green-smeared face and was smiling like the Lotus Contemplative, without showing his teeth. They were barely visible in the dark, standing next to a streak of phosphorescent fungus.

"I've found the way out," Bar-Woten said. "Due north. No troops surrounding the forest, no one to block our way."

Kiril said he felt ashamed the soldiers of Mediweva were so incompetent. Bar-Woten laughed softly and guided him by the shoulder to a narrow natural path.

"Where did Barthel go? I saw him drop," Kiril said.

"Into a ditch," Barthel said. "Tumbled me about, put the horse on its back and spilled the supplies. But I gathered them up, pulled the horse to its side and kept it quiet until I could hear what was going on. The Bey came to tell me all was clear but to be quiet."

"Orders still stand," Bar-Woten said.

They left the forest in a few minutes and rode across fields of wild oats. When morning caught them they were riding hard for the north and the borders of Mundus Lucifa.

Four

The countryside of Mediweva was slowly changing its character. Lowlands and plains gave way to high, craggy peaks and green river courses. Forests became thinner and scrubby; green turned sere. The air grew cool. And still they were pursued.

The parties trailing them had given up steam vehicles. Now the chase was mounted and on foot. Bar-Woten figured it wouldn't end with the border of Mundus Lucifa, either — Ibisians, rumored or otherwise, were not popular in any land. So he stripped off all signs of his past twenty years and gathered together the accouterments of a mountain traveler — animal-skin clothes from the game they shot, rough bark fabric sewn together with the fibers of spear-tipped succulents, a collection of furs over his shoulder. Barthel put aside his Ibisian clothes and went nearly naked like an aborigine from Pashkesh — a role he could mimic well enough by simply down-grading his Arbuck tongue to grunts and slides. Kiril remained a penitent and replaced his cat with the remnants of a hide Bar-Woten had tossed aside.

The trio moved rapidly and efficiently, never so fast as to wear their horses down. They were in generally unpopulated countryside. Replacing good mounts would be difficult.

Because they frequently took cuts across rivers and over fields of smoothed rock and sand, they threw off their searchers for hours at a stretch, and thus moved faster. The

border of Mundus Lucifa grew close — a hundred kilometers, fifty, ten. Then they crossed it — a low barbed wire
strand posted with wood and stone markers.

As they prepared to stop and hide for the night, Barthel's
horse went lame. He examined the beast's foreleg and found
a splintered river stone had wedged into the hoof, splitting it
to the quick. Left alone, the beast could hobble about and
feed off the grassland well enough — but it couldn't be
ridden. And it wouldn't be able to move fast enough to keep
up with them.

Their supplies were low. There was little to transfer from
horse to horse. They buried the saddle in a wadi as the sky
was graying. Rain would fall before darkness came — and
the wadi would fill with water, likely to cover their traces.

They found a pile of rocks firmly mounted against the
floods and higher than the water was likely to rise. After
checking it out for vermin, they rigged a hidden shelter and
rested, waiting for the storm to break.

The front of rain hit with the impact of a spilled bucket.
Rivers grew in minutes, carried away whole landscapes as
mud and scum, and rushed into the wadi. The search party
below faced serious danger of drowning unless they could
find high ground and wait out the storm.

When daylight came the land was still as death. The grass
had been pounded into a thick yellow mud. Water dripped
from the rocks. No wind blew, no animals called, nothing
moved.

The land dropped away ahead of them. Kiril had a
dizzying premonition — where night was a river? — and
looked into the canyon. It was a sheer drop of at least a
kilometer to a series of declines and gorges running helter-
skelter into the grandest chasm he had ever seen. It seemed
to plunge forever into a murky, mist-filled shadow that
complained from far away with a tinny grumble. This was

the natural border of Mundus Lucifa. But Kiril had heard of a way across. They rode and walked gingerly along the canyon's rim for the rest of the day trying to spot the formation he described. Night gloomed up again, and with it came mists and fogs which filled the canyon and wafted at the brim like a ghost ocean.

It was well into the afternoon of the next day before the vapors burned off. Then they saw what Kiril had told them to look for — a monumental rock bridge. It was at least three days away, but they could see its four arches in the distance like the doors to a Mediwevan church. Bar-Woten nodded grimly, satisfied he was seeing a true wonder. Barthel took it in stride. "Allah never surprises me," he said tersely.

Bar-Woten declared they had thrown their pursuers off. "The flood probably convinced them we weren't worth the effort. Either that or it killed them."

"Did you kill any?" Kiril asked. Barthel looked at him sharply, sensing trouble.

"No," Bar-Woten said. "I didn't. I doubt if Barthel did — he was too busy keeping his horse quiet. Did you?"

"No," Kiril said. "I'm not sure I could have."

"The Bey is ashamed that I didn't kill?" Barthel asked grudgingly.

"Not at all. It accomplishes nothing. A skillful hunter kills only for food — and we weren't in the circumstances to enjoy tall pig."

Kiril trudged across the hard-baked stone and mud of the canyon edge. Barthel took his turn on the horse.

"The Ibisians must have thought differently about killing at one time," Kiril said.

"They did," Bar-Woten said. "I did, too."

They switched, and Bar-Woten walked in silence. Birds wheeled over the canyon, wings wide and dark. Their cries counterpointed grumbling from the chasm. To the south the white line of Obelisk Tara still gave a point of reference. It would be thousands of kilometers away before they lost sight of it, and by that time they'd have another Obelisk to follow. There would be the usual region where the sky was darker and the air cooler, then another land with its own spire. But they'd have to cross Mundus Lucifa first, and it had no Obelisk. Bar-Woten asked Kiril what he knew about Mundus Lucifa.

"There are two parts, north and south. I only know about the south. It's a monarchy, fairly backward. A series of fortresses, usually with towns inside, with high mountains and many bridges. They're friendly with Mediweva, but not too friendly. Reluctant to advance their thought. They won't allow anyone to read Obelisk texts, so any knowledge they have is from the past — over two thousand years ago — or rediscovered independently. I've only met a few, none from this far east. They're a handsome, stubborn people."

"Momad?" Barthel asked.

"No. Not Kristian, either. They worship a pantheon not mentioned on the Obelisk — not so far as we've read, anyway."

"Well and good," Bar-Woten said. "Perhaps we can learn something from them — how much the Obelisks make us what we are. Sulay would have enjoyed the opportunity to investigate that. All the lands we passed through believed in the Obelisks. We had to make our own atlases as we traveled. No books were allowed that did not faithfully reprint the Obelisk texts or conservatively comment on what they said. And there are no maps of Hegira on the Obelisks."

"Can I see a map?" Kiril asked. "And an atlas?" He snapped his fingers. "I once read a book that mentions them. Atlas was a god — he held up Earth on his shoulders before Newton and Kopernick destroyed him."

Bar-Woten pulled a square of parchment from his shoulder

42

bag and handed it to Kiril. "Careful with it. It may be the only surviving record of what our geometers and geographers learned. It's a map of what we saw on our March from Ibis."

Kiril unfolded it gingerly, trying to stay balanced on the horse. It was a network of lines and fields of color with shading and odd marks. He could read the names well enough — Obelisk script was universal, so people who believed in Obelisks could always read each other's alphabets — but their positions and other signs meant nothing to him. He had never bothered to read the Obelisk texts that discussed cartography — they seemed useless intellectual exercises, since no such maps existed on Hegira, and Earth was something of a myth.

"Pretty," he said. He folded it and handed it to Bar-Woten, who patiently refolded it and put it in his bag.

"There's something in the canyon," Barthel said. He pointed. Kilometers below lay a crumpled mass which at one time could have been a cylinder. The area around it was too rugged to allow easy access. It looked undisturbed.

"Two or three hundred meters long," Bar-Woten said. "Made of metal. Look how the sun glints off it. Do you know what it is?"

Kiril shook his head, no. He was frowning.

"Could be . . . like the rockets of Khem," Barthel said. "Same shape, only bigger."

"Gun powder would never lift that monster," Bar-Woten said. "It must be a building. Someone put it together and it was destroyed by a rock slide."

But Kiril saw the gouged scar that trailed behind the wreck. He had read a text on missiles and other terrestrial weapons of war — the things on which the First-born had planned to ride away from Earth. "It's a rocket of a kind," he said. He explained what he knew about them, and Bar-Woten raised his eyebrows appreciatively.

43

"I'd like to know who could build something like that," he said.

"Not the Lucifans." Kiril threw a small pebble into the canyon and rose from his knees. "It must have come from very far away. And it was no weapon — it didn't explode."

"That doesn't mean it wasn't a weapon. I understand the Obelisks say not all things explode by fire."

"True," Kiril agreed. "But we have yet to run into explanations for those passages. We accept by faith."

"I think someone else needs no faith. They have proof."

They were some twenty kilometers from the rock bridge when they made camp and bedded down for the night. Dark, heavy clouds roiled above the gray mountains beyond the canyon. Rain splattered on them as they ate their dinner of dried fish and fruit, and later as they slept. When morning cast a pale orange light on their faces the air had chilled considerably, and light specks of snow drifted down. They could not see across the canyon. The river in the chasm bellowed distantly as they mounted. Barthel walked first.

They reached the rock bridge by midafternoon. Few people traveled this route, Kiril said. Commerce was carried on much farther west, where the canyon was swallowed up by a lush rain forest and the river went underground.

Like ants on a highway, the three began the trek across the bridge. The slope to either side was imperceptible, but it eventually rounded smoothly into the sheer walls. At least four holes had been scoured into the sides of the bridge to emerge near the middle. Wind whistled through them with a fierce, mournful tone. When Kiril peered into one, the draft lifted the neck of his cloak up and batted it like a sail.

"Wind and water did this," Bar-Woten said. "Hegira has to have been here for millions of years."

"Been here?" Kiril asked. "Ah, if you're going to be profound, where is here?"

"Wherever, it is not the land of the First-born. It has no stars, no sun, and no moons. Scrittori, can your learning explain that?"

"Of course not."

"That's what I'd like to explain."

Barthel said nothing, but looked down the length of the canyon into gray shadow. Light never reached down there. The shadows were always the same. That seemed important, but he didn't mention it.

By dark they were across the bridge. They camped again, ate, and slept until morning.

Five

Kiril pondered Bar-Woten's quest as the nearest mountains of Mundus Lucifa lowered like black giants through their clouds. Whatever the Ibisian learned, the Obelisks wouldn't help him — that Kiril knew as certainly as he knew he had two arms.

The Obelisks were an enigma unchanged across the history of the Second-born. They were about a thousand kilometers tall, a kilometer across each side and as perfectly square as anyone could measure. They vanished in the endless blue during the daytime and dimly reflected the light of the fire doves at night, rising until the eye couldn't trace them. Entire civilizations were indelibly etched on their faces: histories and philosophies and literatures, records of the home of the First-born called Earth. The arrangement of the texts by subject and date was seemingly random, but a rough progression existed — the higher one read, the more advanced in time and technology the records were. The highest the readers had ever gone in Ibis had been ten kilometers, using balloons like the readers in Mediweva and Khem.

"From each you shall choose the flavor of your birth," the first text on each Obelisk read, "the time of your time, the words you will speak and things you adore. All other things will be as nothing to you."

All Obelisks were the same. The civilizations of Hegira were not. That, Kiril's teachers had told him, was what the

Obelisks meant. All shall choose differently from the texts, climb high or low depending on their technology, to pick what they need from the immortal needles.

They were the only things on Hegira that could be relied upon. All else — penitents, armies, generals, and servants alike — were inconsiderable. Humans twinkled brief as candles. Obelisks stayed.

"What do you want to know?" Kiril asked Bar-Woten.

"Anything concrete. I'll feast on crumbs if I have to."

"The Bey knows about its name, Hegira," Barthel said. "It refers to the flight of Momad from Mecca, among the First-born. The Qur'an tells many such wonderful tales. Not Yesu, not the Lotus Contemplative, nor any other can claim that namesake — not even, pardon my obstinance, Bey — Eloshim."

"I'd never heard of Ibis before your armies came. How far did you travel to get here?"

"Fifty thousand kilometers."

"How did you measure it?"

"The angle of the Obelisks to each other, triangulating and assuming five thousand kilometers between each Obelisk. We would pick a point on the Obelisk line and set that as our triangle apex — "

Kiril interrupted. "So you crossed how many degrees . . . say, between the Obelisk in Ibis and the Obelisk Tara?"

"You mean?"

"How many degrees would they be apart if they could make an angle?"

"Ah," Bar-Woten understood. "Twenty-three degrees."

"Did your geometers decide that Hegira was round?"

"It was round as far as they could measure. Of course there was no way of knowing if we were merely going up a gigantic hill fifty thousand kilometers across. But we couldn't

47

see distant lands by looking at the sky, no matter where we were. So we assumed Hegira was round."

"Then there's a way of figuring out how big across it is."

"Two hundred and forty-nine thousand kilometers."

Kiril looked down at the Ibisian, his mouth working to repeat the figure. He could hardly grasp it. He sighed and shook his head. "It's imponderable. Earth was nowhere near that large. Some stars were that size. They were supposed to be the fiercest things imaginable."

"Then Hegira may be a star."

"I don't think so," Kiril said. "I didn't study the texts too heavily when I copied them, but an object the size of a star would hold us to the ground like ghosts to a funeral stone."

"Gravity."

"Even if it isn't a star, though, Hegira must be very light, or it would hold us as strongly. Perhaps it's hollow."

"And we are on the outside."

"If the Obelisks lean away from each other, that would seem to be true. And as you say, we don't see distant lands when we look at the sky."

"Perhaps Allah meant it to be imponderable," Barthel offered.

"Allah, as you say, gave us brains to think and solve," Bar-Woten said.

Another question bothered Kiril. If the armies of Ibis had discovered so many wondrous things, why did they leave a bloody swath wherever they went? He couldn't put the concepts of barbarians and scholars in one package. He opened his mouth to talk about it, then shut it grimly. He knew so little about the men he was traveling with. Better to keep his peace and see what they offered to tell first.

A shiver made his hands falter. "Why?" he asked himself

silently. "Why have I delivered myself to wolves?" Then, glancing upward covertly, "Why have You?"

Because he loved. His love would not stop clawing the inside of his chest and burning fires beneath his brain. Move, it demanded. And he moved.

Six

"It's called the Uhuru Massif," Kiril said. "There should be a few small towns and forts here, but I don't see any."

"They could be hidden in the ridges and valleys," Bar-Woten said. "I don't see any roads. No trails."

"No commerce comes this way from Mediweva. There may not be any."

"Have you ever talked with Lucifans?" the Ibisian asked.

"Not often. I was very young when we went to the western end. They don't trust Obelisk nations very much."

"They feel deprived, hm?"

Barthel countered strongly. "Perhaps they feel we are misled. There is much that is doubtful on the Obelisks."

Bar-Woten nodded and pursed his lips. "We'll probably meet any greeting parties where the two plateaus divide, in the cleft between. If you say they're not usually hostile, we shouldn't greet them with drawn weapons. But no polite society will resent our hands on the hilts."

Kiril walked beside the Ibisian's horse as they approached the cleft. A small stream trickled muddily down the middle of the wadi, but grotesque ridges and rills running parallel to it suggested this was a powerful watercourse when rains cascaded from the mountain slopes. The horses picked their way cautiously over the rugged ground. Bar-Woten kept his eyes on the pillars of scoured soft stone walling the gorge on both sides. They were near the bluff below the plateau flats when voices called out. Their owners couldn't be seen.

"*Ua hight thee?*" one asked.

Kiril frowned, trying to understand the dialect from his studies of Obelisk English. He knew the word *hight*. From that he pieced together the rest. "We are three from Mediweva," he answered. "*Trithi de Mediweva!*"

They continued climbing until they were level with the plateau. Behind a ridge of rocks ahead three faces peered at them. "Your purpose!" one demanded.

"To travel through Mundus Lucifa. We are scholars."

"Your studies?"

"Folklore," Bar-Woten undertoned, looking down at his saddlebags and rearranging them nonchalantly.

"Folklore and myth!" Kiril answered.

"What would Obeliskers want with an ignorant land?"

"Natural truth," he answered, hoping to guess the correct response to the formula. They weren't dealing with simple barbarians. The border guards to Mundus Lucifa were specially trained and erudite.

"Come forward. You have papers?"

The Lucifan's Mediwevan was excellent. He had no accent.

"No papers," Kiril said. "Our studies aren't condoned in Mediweva. We don't use the Obelisk texts."

Two sets of three horsemen galloped from both sides to ride as escort. The three behind the ridge emerged and walked to meet the strangers. The guards wore carefully beaded buskins, patchwork leather leggings, sporranlike pouches, and metal skullcaps engraved with designs in an alphabet Kiril didn't recognize. Their shirts were khaki with square, puffed pockets. Bandoliers hung from their shoulders and supported pouches and scabbards at their waists.

"You've traveled far?" the leader asked. He was a short, stocky man with a booming voice.

"Across the chasm," Kiril said, gesturing behind them.

51

The men were tall and dark, except for their leader; almost olive-colored, their skin shining like old leather. Their eyes were white as talc with enormous blue or green pupils. All in all, Bar-Woten decided, they were as handsome a group of men as any he'd met on the March.

"Ah," the leader said, nodding his head. "Then you saw the thing at the bottom. You think we built that?"

"No," Kiril said.

The guard looked insulted, but finally grinned and shrugged his shoulders. "The Mediwevans didn't?"

"I doubt it," Kiril said, laughing.

"The old scholars drove you out of the country then, hm?" He shifted subjects without blinking.

"In a manner of speaking."

The guards whispered to each other. The six men on horseback watched the intruders silently. Kiril felt sweat forming on his back. "Listen," the leader said, "not many people come through this way, and we wonder why you do. You have an excuse, but there's trouble in your country now. So you'll be taken to the city ahead and our superiors will decide what should be done. Follow my men, please." They crossed the plateau and took an old trail around an escarpment of weathered granite rock.

Each escort wore a different insignia on the ribbon that secured his skullcap. One bore a coiled snake surrounding a clutch of eggs; another a hawk with wings spread; and a third a rosette of spiked red petals. Three of the horsemen left them at the top of the ridge and rode to the west. The remaining ensigns talked among themselves as they paced, ignoring the intruders.

The Lucifan with the rosette pointed down the smoothly paved road and said, "Ubidharm." Coming around a sandy hummock covered with thorny bushes, they had their first view of a Lucifan city.

It was small but impressive. The architecture was predominantly stone, which was to be expected from the landscape. Walls three times as high as a man curved and snaked around the inner city, which rose from numerous hills like a display of stone drinking cups and hourglasses. Bar-Woten spotted an aqueduct plunging in a straight line from a snow-hatted peak. It was large enough to satisfy this town, certainly, and several more like it. The water rushed over baffles in the stone run and glistened with white foam.

Kiril had seen similar architecture years before as a child on his short journey to the western border of Mundus Lucifa. But it had been scrubby and undisciplined compared to this. The walls were painted in browns and earth greens with intricate mandalas, highlighted by hemispheres of white marble as big as a man's head. Red sandstone crenels topped the walls, capped by balls of gray granite expertly cut and polished. The city within was a complete contrast to the smoke-stained buildings of Madreghb. Brilliant white-washed masonry and plaster caught cloud-filtered, greenish mountain light and stood out like snow against the black volcanic rock. The glare was dazzling. Beyond the walls on all sides natural protrusions of stone hid Ubidharm from view of all but the highest peaks.

Barthel looked it over with gaping delight. "Some cities in Khem were like this," he told Kiril in a hushed voice. "Holy places where prophets lived."

The gates of Ubidharm were open, lightly guarded by a few men dressed like the escorts. They passed through the outer village, a hundred-meter stretch of low mud and brick buildings dun-colored, neat but unimpressive; then under the corbel arch of the gate. They stopped at a red brick structure, which Kiril guessed was a custom house, or a guard station, or both.

They were signaled to dismount and go into the station.

53

The interior was square and clean with a polished slate floor and furniture made of rugged wood and rattan. The officer of the guard — without a skull-cap, but wearing a green sash around his neck like a prelate — looked them over noncommittally and spoke to the escorts. He took the guard with the rosette into a separate room.

They returned a moment later, and the officer extended his right hand to Barthel, apparently starting with the darkest and working down. "Welcome to the Land of Light," he said. He was tall and black with a bristling moustache and a head shaved clean but for three closely braided stripes running from nape to crown. "Who leads this party?" He looked at Barthel expectantly. The young man stammered and was about to point to Bar-Woten.

"No one," the Ibisian answered. "We travel as equals. We appreciate your welcome."

"I hear you are scholars of the Obelisks — readers, I take it?"

Kiril decided a modified sort of truth was best. "I'm a reader," he said. "A scrittori, actually. But we haven't come here to preach."

"No." The officer went to a heavy wooden cabinet with thin horizontal drawers and opened one. He pulled out a short stack of forms and took a reed pen from a cup on the desk. "I'll have to know your purpose in the Land of Light. Your names, where you are from — Pashkesh, am I correct?" he asked Barthel. The Khemite nodded. "And where you intend to go within the country. Few Mediwevans cross this part of the border. None for at least five years. And some — ah — Ibisians have escaped here recently. Thirty or forty in fact."

Bar-Woten nodded casually. "We heard of the final purge," he said. "Where a river runs to ground, some drops must escape."

54

"A particularly foul and nasty river, too." The officer's eyes examined him closely. "What were you in Mediweva, sir?"

"A balloonwright. I took my learning in Minora, outside Madreghb, and left with my companions to avoid — " he hemmed, "rigid thinking."

"We have sympathy for the Obeliskers," the officer said, scribing away at one of the forms. "No understanding, perhaps, but sympathy. We do not fear preachers here. Usually they are the ones with something to fear. The people of Ubidharm are mountainfolk; and insular, proud. Missionaries who are obnoxious pass through rapidly if they pass at all. We must often apologize to their homelands."

The forms were already translated, and it took them only a few minutes to fill in the required information. The official paperwork was brief. When it was over a short oath was administered — in dialect, then in translation — and they were given cards.

"You will report to the gatehouse of each city or town you visit. There aren't many here — but if you go west you will need identification. If you plan to cross the mountains and go north you will probably have to register again — I don't know. Northern Land of Light is very different from the south. And I wouldn't recommend crossing now. It's rugged travel. We won't have you followed, but we have a good semaphore system. Any trouble and we send out troops, not always with pleasant results. We trust, though, you are honest men. Be discreet — I repeat we are insular — and please follow the basics of cleanliness. I'm sure the Pashkesher will be able to inform you what they are." Barthel nodded vigorously.

They left the gatehouse and their horses were returned to them. Bar-Woten saw the saddlebags had been searched. He had expected it — the map was in his shirt pocket. Perhaps they wouldn't have understood it — or, being non-Obeliskers, perhaps there were no rulings on maps and they would have. Either way he had taken no chances. He was surprised to find they'd been allowed to keep their pistols.

The city was pleasant, with narrow alleys and streets bricked and tarred, sidewalks of freshly scrubbed tile, and slatted wood window louvers painted clear, bright colors. It was so different from Madreghb as to make Bar-Woten draw a deep breath, as if he were in open country again. "You seem to know a little of the patois," he said to Kiril. "How much?"

"Very little. It was mentioned in secondary training as an offshoot of several Obelisk languages — chiefly Old French and East Midlands dialect in English. They read the Obelisks ages ago, in the Prime Epoch, but isolated themselves here later."

Bar-Woten looked impressed. "You really were a diligent scrittori, weren't you?" he said. "There's a lot you can teach us."

Kiril smiled warily but said nothing.

Southern Mundus Lucifa was barely a hundred kilometers wide, most of it mountains and high plateaus. Kiril had no idea how many cities there were, or what would be the easiest route to cross. "Maybe we should ask," he said. Bar-Woten nodded, took Kiril's mount by the reins, and led them through the gate-street.

A faint drizzle fell, mixed with snowflakes as wide as butterflies. The greenish air between the mountains indicated night would be coming within the hour. But Bar-Woten didn't stop at the inns along the street. He seemed to be looking for something else. His route took them through the more hidden recesses of the town.

Barthel was stonily quiet, not unhappy, but keeping a close watch on Kiril. This made the Mediwevan nervous. He concentrated on the carved stonework and tile that covered the walls. The designs weren't markedly different from such work in Madreghb. The predominant patterns were flowerlike, rosettes and intricate daisy chains that made the closed eye spin. Increasingly, however, the walls were the same whitewash as the upper floors, or ocher mud-brick sealed with a waxy varnish.

Bar-Woten leaned forward in his saddle and peered down the street with his single eye. The street sloped at a twenty-degree angle down to a courtyard wet with rain and slush. They were almost soaked through and Kiril was getting angry.

"Barthel?" the Ibisian asked.

"That is one, Bey," Barthel answered. Bar-Woten grunted and nodded, spurring his horse ahead.

"I'd thought they were everywhere, until I couldn't find one in Mediweva," he said. "Strange country your people keep, friend."

"One what?" Kiril asked.

Barthel smiled and pointed. The closed windows surrounding the courtyard were painted an ageless red. A ponchoed, drowsing livery boy sat next to an open stable door from which a warm glow issued. They could smell fodder and animals. The boy sat up at their approach, rubbing his eyes and looking them over imperturbably. He greeted them and took the two horses by their reins. Bar-Woten purveyed Mediwevan scrip, which the boy looked at closely, then accepted.

"We'll stay here tonight and relax," the Ibisian told Kiril. "I don't know what your creed says about such things, but a country without one of these is hardly civilized."

"One of what?" He looked up at the windows on the second floor and saw a bosomy girl lean out, dark as midnight, with hair braided in circular ringlets, her teeth gleaming like lanterns between pink lips.

"Oh." Kiril pulled on his horse's reins in surprise, jerking them from the stable boy's grip. The animal reared back. "O-o-oh! One of *those*!" He wheeled the animal around, trying to control it, and the courtyard filled with clopping and whinnying. The stable boy grabbed the halter and let him dismount. "We can't rest here," Kiril said loudly. "Why should we rest here?"

Bar-Woten walked with a heavy, water-splashing tread to the large wooden door of the inn. "You may sleep with the horses if you want."

Kiril was furious. This was worse, in its own way, than finding his companions were thieves and murderers. They were whore patrons! He ran after them, but stopped at the open doorway, weaving back and forth, trying to decide whether to follow or stay outside. The cold and wet decided for him. He stood on the threshold, mouth agape, as he saw the Ibisian and the Khemite enter an incense-filled room beyond a round doorway. Dark tapestries with suggestive designs hung in the anteroom. He didn't want to stay there. "Wait!"

Bar-Woten removed his cloak and smiled at a young woman dressed in a straight black dress. Red flower designs rimmed her dress's sleeves and hem. Though he couldn't have known her language, communication passed easily enough between them. Barthel carried his own coat on one arm and looked around the room with the same subdued smile he'd worn earlier. Kiril joined them reluctantly, unable to say anything intelligent and afraid to make a fool of himself.

Bar-Woten's woman — lighter in color than the one who'd leaned over the sill in the courtyard — took him by the arm and led him up the stairs to the second floor. A second girl appeared from another room and took Barthel. None appeared for Kiril. He felt left out and relieved at the same time; but why had he been ignored? What part of the ritual had he failed to observe? His face burned, and he held his hands up to feel his forehead. He was hot, as if he'd whipped himself into a fever again.

He sat alone in the darkened room and fumed. Finally a small child — he couldn't tell if it was a boy or a girl — came up behind him and sat next to him on the bench. "*Ama sol?*" it asked. He thought that over and decided the child was asking if he wanted a room. He nodded. The child took him by the hand and led him up the stairs. For a moment he was frightened he was getting involved in something far worse than what Bar-Woten and Barthel had chosen, but he relaxed when a bare, comfortable-looking room was shown to him, empty of companionship. He thanked the child and went to the small, clean bed to sit and think.

Bar-Woten squatted in the dark with his girl beside him, listening to her snores. A fire dove's faint light came through a window high in the wall and threw a bluish square on the carpeted and pillowed floor. He ran his hand over the girl's shoulder and she hissed in her sleep. His hair rose for a moment, the reaction was so alien — to grunt or grumble but not to hiss! Then he lay back on the hard stone neck rest. His nose itched with incense. It had been a year since he'd last lain with a female. The smell of her body, as sweet (because she was a vegetarian) as that of a horse, had maddened him, and he'd taken her several times, almost furiously, each time facing her calm, restrained smile with a wide single-eyed grimace.

The rain returned to patter at the window. A squabble between birds bounced back and forth in the courtyard, spears and arrows of song.

He slept.

Barthel, in another room, kept his girl awake explaining the Faith of Prophets to her. She listened with stifled yawns and good humor until dawn, understanding nothing, then put her hand over his mouth, pushed him gently back into the mattress, and went to sleep sitting up. Her eyes closed, her body drooped ever so slightly, and her breathing became easier. Barthel watched with wide eyes, haunted and delighted, then flopped back and giggled in the dawn glow. Allah, that had been fine! Hours with *houris* were never wasted. Especially if they were so close to being Momadans anyway, that only the words differed.

Mundus Lucifa was a friendly land, if insular.

Seven

Snow covered the courtyard and old men in yellow jackets with loose black pants pushed it around with brooms and shovels. Water sloshed in their wake; it was a half-hearted snow and would be melted by midday. Bar-Woten watched from the high window, standing on tiptoe on a wooden bench. Something bustled behind him, and he turned to face a parade, one child carrying a tray of food, one girl with another, Barthel with a robe wrapped around him, and Kiril dressed as if he were ready to leave.

The girl and the child exited, chattering to each other and carrying the empty trays. Barthel and Kiril sat down to the meal, and Bar-Woten kneeled beside them on a low stool. The covered ceramic bowls steamed, and hot liquid — a thick, buttery tea — piped in its valved pot. They set to eating without a word. Kiril looked between them with a fixed, accusing expression. The Ibisian finished his first bowl and wiped his mouth with a lap towel. He frowned and stared at Kiril.

"Okay," he said. "You're unhappy. What are you unhappy about?"

"Your behavior."

"You're our keeper, no? Self-appointed?"

"I don't understand why you engage in a debauch as soon as you enter a foreign land. There aren't any brothels in Mediweva, and with good reason. They're an affront to human dignity and God's law."

"Kristians generally object to love," Barthel told Bar-Woten around a bite of bread.

"Not at all! We object to the profanation of the spiritual body of the woman."

"I profaned nothing; I exchanged. I did justice by the girl — so did Barthel, I hope. You should have too. It would have cleared anxieties from your soul."

"That's barbaric! I was starting to think Ibis must have been civilized, if not Sulay's armies, but now I'm not so sure!"

"To paraphrase the Obelisks, each to his own fashion. I have been holding within for a year, Barthel as long. It does no good to hold within for such a time."

Kiril turned to the Khemite. "You're a Momadan, you should know the Prophet forbids such actions."

"Then why is Paradise equipped with such pleasures for the faithful? Momad forbade those excesses that would weaken the body and prevent his people from performing their duties on Earth."

Kiril shook his head. "It is a sin!"

"I don't understand the word," Bar-Woten said.

"You wouldn't. Not with the conscience of thousands of murders — how many rapes, how many debauches without payment?"

The Ibisian put down his lap towel and reached across with a broad, wiry hand to grab Kiril's lapels. "I grudge no one's beliefs, but no one judges me. So I am a devil. I've been told that many times. I have never stolen or raped. I have never dishonored in battle. That could not be said for all Ibisians. I may be evil, but my evil has yet to rot my standards. Understand? It may eat at me every day, but the fiber remains, and I intend to purge myself with the knowledge we find. My crimes are my own concern." He let Kiril go and cursed under his breath. "Eat, don't talk."

Kiril sat trembling and wild-eyed at the table for a long breath, then stood and walked out. Barthel looked after him sympathetically and suggested the Bey shouldn't have lost his temper.

"He's young," Bar-Woten said. "I'll apologize when he's ready but I won't beg forgiveness."

Kiril ran to the end of the hall trying not to listen to the sounds that came from a few of the rooms. He walked stiffly down the stairs into the foyer, then stomped through the anteroom and stood in the slushy courtyard, trying to decide what to do. He had had enough of his own insanity.

The livery boy brought his horse out for him upon request and helped him adjust the saddle. Kiril didn't care if the others were going to be left with fewer provisions. "Let them spend their money on that instead of another debauch!" he whispered harshly to himself. The boy looked up at him with curious eyes. "*Vasheesh?*" he asked in the Pashkesh tongue — a tip?

"*Mafeesh*," Kiril answered. "My pockets are empty."

He spurred his horse forward and left the courtyard.

Horses were crowding the crest of the road. Kiril stopped short at the bottom of the inclined street. In front of the horses stumbled a party of bloody and tattered men in white uniforms, much like what he had first seen Bar-Woten wearing. The drive was heading in his direction, right for the courtyard. The men on horseback were Mediwevan.

The purge had crossed the border. The Holy Pontiff was running his quarry to ground even in foreign fields.

Shouts arose when they spotted him. "Stop!" And a shot rang out. For a long, paralyzed moment he stood his ground, wanting to cry out that he was one of them, that he was a Mediwevan. But he knew it was crazy to face them even as an accomplice. His insanity had come to the only possible end.

63

He pulled his horse around and galloped back into the courtyard. "Bar-Woten!" he called. "Barthel! Mount up! They're here!"

He saw the Ibisian's face in a small window on the second floor. He disappeared. Barthel replaced him. "Bring out the other horse!" the Khemite ordered.

Kiril dismounted and stopped. How long would it take the soldiers to get to the bottom of the street with men running before them? "Kristos!" he panted. He ran to the stables, pushed the boy aside, and knocked his hand on the beam beside each stall, trying to find the other horse. It was still blanketed but unsaddled. "The saddle!" he shouted to the boy. "The saddle!"

"*Mafeesh*," the boy answered in a falsetto, waggling his hips. "*Bastardi!*"

Kiril threw open the stall door and avoided the animal's tentative back-kick, whapping it across the nose with the flat of his hand to make it behave. He pushed it out of the stall and breathed his thanks it was still haltered. The Ibisian ran into the stables with clothes dangling and took the horse from him. Kiril spied the saddle on a rack, whipped it off with surprising strength, and tossed it on the ground beside the horse. "Is there time?" Bar-Woten asked.

"How the hell should I know?" Kiril shouted.

He walked backward from the stable trying to keep his eyes on all things at once — the saddling, the courtyard, the frightened-looking stable boy who had stepped into more trouble than he'd expected. Kiril stumbled in his crabwise gait and fell on his side and hands, scraping himself and wetting his clothes. Cursing, he stood up again and ran into the doorway of the brothel. Girls and old men and women were flooding the anteroom. He couldn't break through the crowd. "I have the bags!" Barthel called from the other side.

"Then come this side with them for God's sake!"

The Khemite pushed and kicked his way through. He emerged with the leather pouches and they turned to the courtyard. They were just in time to see the chained Ibisians being shoved ahead of the mounted troops. The press of the crowd in the room behind pushed the two into the courtyard like corks from a bottle. The wet stones were suddenly crowded with running, shrieking whores. The Ibisian prisoners backed off as though they'd stepped in a nest of ants. The horses of their captors reared and plunged. The archway to the courtyard was a chaos of neighing animals and shouting men.

Bar-Woten rode out of the stable with his pistol in one hand. "Mount up!" he shouted to Kiril. "Get the other horse!" he told Barthel. Kiril took his offered hand, slipped on the stirrup, and nearly fell on his back, but found himself lifted bodily with great strain on his arm into the saddle, where the hard leather curve put excruciating pressure on his groin. To make it worse, Bar-Woten kicked the horse forward.

The courtyard had a small gate in the rear, barely tall enough for a riderless horse. The Ibisian headed for that, and Barthel followed. Kiril swung down only too gladly to open the latch. Then, remounting and hanging over the side, he plunged with the Ibisian through the gate into an alleyway crowded with gawking Lucifans. "Aside!" Bar-Woten shouted. "Aside, damn you!"

Behind them the troops found themselves mired in stumbling, groaning prisoners and screaming women. The Grand Pimp, splendid in his flowing red and gold robes, came out briefly to see what the confusion was, gawped and ran back to his inner office.

The alley opened onto another street paralleling the main boulevard. They turned on it and rode as fast as they could, scattering pedestrians and sidestepping carts. Kiril looked back and saw a pair of Mediwevans leap from a sidestreet and ride hard after. "They're all behind us!" he cried out. Bar-Woten shook his head angrily and turned onto another street, then around to the gate thoroughfare. "I hope that confuses them," he called back to Kiril.

Kiril looked behind. He couldn't see anyone but Barthel. The gate ahead looked calm. The custom house had two guards standing idly in front, smoking long-handled pipes and talking. They saw the riders galloping toward them and ran inside to grab weapons, but the two horses were out the gate before they could return. More soldiers mounted and followed, almost colliding with their colleagues, who had tracked the chase back to the gate after the detour.

A dirt road ran around the outside of the huts clustered below the walls. They followed it, still riding at bone-jarring speed, and rounded the first major curve of the wall. Barthel called from behind. "They're following!"

In five minutes, they were on the north side of Ubidharm. Their luck was holding — a broad, well-paved road led away from the city, skirted the aqueduct, and rose into the northern mountains of the Uhuru Massif. The riders behind gave up in a few kilometers. The Mediwevans couldn't get out of the city gates — front or rear — before the chase was futile.

Bar-Woten slowed his pace after diverting them onto a dirty byroad. They dismounted next to a tumbling snow stream and walked the horses until they were calm and less heated. They watered them sparingly. Bar-Woten then let Kiril ride as he ran beside for a few kilometers.

Their prospects on the road ahead — with depleted supplies and sparse countryside — were not cheering. Barthel counted the rounds of ammunition in the pistols and the two boxes they had purchased in Mediweva. They had a little over sixty rounds and seven arrows to fit a fold-up bow that

66

had been part of Bar-Woten's kit. "We're going to be limited," Kiril said when the count was finished.

"We won't be able to fight it out if that's a thing to worry about," Bar-Woten agreed. "But I'm a fair shot with a pistol. Yourself?"

"An amateur," Kiril said. "You were stupid to take me along. What good can I do you?"

"You'll prove your importance in time," Bar-Woten said. They mounted again.

"I'll just have to grow up a little, hm?" He said it angrily, flushing at the thought that this man would think him immature. Bar-Woten didn't answer.

The road turned from a defile into a ledge, following the circumference of a wedge-shaped peak whose cap was lost in cloud. They saw that the main road, now fifty or sixty meters below, came to an abrupt end. "Our luck is holding so far," Bar-Woten said. "Let's hope we don't run out of road this way."

Eight

The Ibisian fell asleep very late, shivering and half-hallucinating fires and warmth. The three huddled together; their blankets kept them from freezing as night temperatures dropped below zero, but didn't keep them comfortable. Bar-Woten slipped in and out of a dream about his father and a trip to the Obelisk in Ibis. As he remembered it, they had passed the lakes whose birds gave Ibis its name, vast seas and clouds of white feathers, and taken the long road through the plantations of Thosala to the spire. In the dream people crowded around the circumference of the spire and stared up. The walls of the Obelisk were covered with writing, his father told him, but as they grew closer and pushed through the crowd — which was filled with mounted Mediwevans looking for children to harass — he saw the wall go blank. "It's a sign," a tall woman near him said. "When the walls go blank it means there are no more reasons for people to exist, because there's nothing left to read."

"The books," Bar-Woten said aloud.

Kiril peered sleepily from his own mummy of blankets.

"No," the woman in the dream said. "They're blank, too. No more reason to read, no more people to read."

The crowds slowly vanished, first legs and arms and then torsos. The heads were the last to go. One head, his father, it seemed (though they were all hairless and hard to recognize), told him the words of the Obelisks still existed in their memories, and they would not be eradicated until they forgot. "No!" he said. "I'm a little boy, I don't know enough to be saved, that can't be the way it is!"

"Then why are you disappearing?" the head said. "Look, all of you is gone now."

Kiril watched the squirming Ibisian and wondered what bloody nightmares he was experiencing. No doubt they were about battles and debauchery. Then he drifted off into his own fitful dreams.

Their trackers never appeared again. For six days they journeyed across the cold passes, and on the morning of the seventh day — which Barthel said was symbolic for Kristians and Momadans — they looked over the side of the road into a broad green valley. Several kilometers below, the rift extended into bluish haze, ending at the shores of the largest body of water they had ever seen. It reached to the horizon, and between distant peaks ahead, they could see its gray-blue line.

From the altitude the valley was a patchwork of farmland and unworked or dormant fields. On the shoreline a city rose. It looked as large as Madreghb.

The land reminded Bar-Woten of Ibis. Near sea level the ground was rich and fertile, and the slopes of the foothills were covered with terraced paddies and forests of camphor-wood and pine. He told them of his days in Ibis — stories Barthel had never heard before — and the memories made him feel warm and mellow. Twenty years of battle, misery, and bloodshed hadn't obscured the joy he had known as a child.

The weather was too warm and pleasant for any of them to feel gloomy. Coming through one last scattered patch of cloud into the valley proper, they chatted cheerfully.

Kiril forgot his distress in Ubidharm. He was somewhat ashamed of his prudery. He talked freely about his training as a scrittori. The balloons and their use along the walls of the Obelisk fascinated Bar-Woten, who asked many questions.

The road had fallen into disrepair in the mountains and was now a token trail with ruts where carts ran. Their horses were sweating and tired, so they stopped in the shade of feathery yellow-green trees near the trail for a brief rest. The wind whistling through the upper branches made Kiril drowsy, but Bar-Woten stayed alert. Barthel suggested a short nap, and Kiril agreed, but the Ibisian stood by the horses looking across the valley. He wanted to avoid more surprises.

After an hour's rest they continued along the farm sideroads until the city was little more than a kilometer away. Barthel examined the valley walls behind them. There was still that connection to make — why were some valleys unlivable to the Faithful? Because the darkness was too deep in them? Why did this valley fill with light and warmth? Others certainly didn't, no matter what season.

They made a small camp as night fell. Kiril greeted a few carriages that rolled past them on the improved roads. They were curious vehicles, orange as a darkling zenith, with glossy lacquer over wood, carved and embellished with inlaid shellwork and covered with a tapestry-like top fringed with tied leather ornaments. The beasts pulling them were not horses, but bluish and horselike with a touch of wild moose. Bar-Woten said he had never seen animals like them. The carriages rattled past, friendly and unconcerned.

The next morning they entered the city and discovered it was named Mur-es-Werd. It was truly a city, not a walled hideaway like Ubidharm. Its commerce extended up and down the coast of the sea for thousands of kilometers. This was the heart and the blood of Mundus Lucifa, then, not the little patch of mountain communities. Kiril had never heard of Mur-es-Werd, nor of the ocean beyond, and his ignorance distressed him. Obviously his life in Mediweva had been extremely insular.

"It's the way with all Obelisk countries," Bar-Woten assured him. "When truth sits in your midst, why search elsewhere?"

"For sheer curiosity," Kiril muttered. "At least what you learn is interesting and tells you more about the Second-born."

"The Second-born don't always want to know more about themselves," Barthel said.

Mur-es-Werd began as a series of vineyards and orchards. Varieties of fruit grew here that they had never seen before. The fields gave way to scattered whitewashed villas and a central stupa topping a gathering place. These in turn gave way to suburban slums with narrow cobbled streets winding every which way like worms trailing through wood. The atmosphere was not one of cleanliness, as in Ubidharm, but of vibrant, rapid life. At times the sanitation was deplorable, but no worse on the whole than in some Mediwevan cities.

Small rocky hills rose in the center of the city, cordoned by the crumbling walls of what must have once been an impressive bastion. A few towers, square and imposing, remained in fair condition. Around these were walled compounds adorned with Lucifan mandalas in stony green and red.

Kiril found his dialect almost useless, since what little he knew was not comparable to the northern patois. They had little trouble, however — tourists were not unknown and not unwelcome either. The shoreline was something of a resort.

By noon they had decided the neighborhoods along the beaches were more suited to them. Curious children crowded around, trying to sell trinkets and stale crullers.

Bar-Woten stopped at a sea wall overlooking the resort beaches. He shaded his eye and looked across the bay, allowing himself a moment of awe. "The ships!" he said. "Look at the ships!"

Barthel followed the Bey's eye and felt his throat catch. They were huge, as graceful as seabirds. He had never seen any larger. He looked at Bar-Woten and knew what the next leg of their journey would be. "I don't even like water, not to swim in," Barthel said quietly. Kiril smiled, then sobered as he caught the Khemite's meaning.

"Over that?" he asked Bar-Woten, pointing at the unimaginable blue-green. The Ibisian nodded.

Nine

Their Mediwevan coins were welcome, but they were fast running out, and as yet they had no way to replace their money. There was also the matter of the sea voyage, which Bar-Woten was talking up more each day. His companions tried to ignore him, but there was no other way to go but across the water. North lay that way, and their way was north.

Their first step was to purchase a number of small, old dictionaries from a bookstore in Mur-es-Werd. Bar-Woten found the decrepit shop fascinating. Kiril was less than charmed. There were dozens of books lying around that he was certain had never come from Obelisk texts — histories of Mundus Lucifa, books of maps, and biographies. It was plainly an unorthodox place.

At night, roomless, they slept on the beach. One always sat guard on a small rock above their adopted spit of sand. The waves sounded like fighting animals up and down the coast. Some were as big as two-story buildings, pouring up between offshore channels of rock and howling across the turbulent sand. At night, when the waves glowed like graceful ghosts, Barthel hid his eyes from the sight and concentrated on the light-scattered city.

Their fourth morning in Mur-es-Werd, Bar-Woten woke to the smell of smoke and saw Kiril fixing a breakfast of fish. A long pole strung with line was stuck in the sand beside

73

him. "I bought it an hour ago," Kiril explained. "More practical than books, no?"

Bar-Woten had been learning the dialect rapidly, much faster than Barthel, and could speak to the Lucifans well enough to be understood. As he ate Kiril's breakfast he wondered out loud why the country was called Mundus Lucifa. Kirl held up his finger to show a pause while he chewed. "Simple enough," he said. "Lightning comes out of the mountains. Some of the storms are frightful." But he'd never actually seen one, other than the rainburst they'd passed through before crossing the chasm.

They made inquiries that day in the shipyards about the need for seamen. The response was discouraging — blank stares and shaking heads. There was a glut on the market. Ten men for every berth. Still, foreign ships coming in frequently had room for new men — usually because a few had been lost at sea.

"The foreign ships won't be as picky about taking on strangers," Bar-Woten said. "We might have a chance with them."

They did odd jobs around the ports, walking from one cluster of docks and yards to another. Kiril had his first taste of heavy physical labor and didn't like it. He resented the Ibisian's stoic indifference to the work.

They lived this way for three weeks. No foreign ships put into port, and no domestic ships put out. The season was difficult for trading. Soon big storms would lash the ocean into strips of wave-wracked lace. Spouts and hurricanes would begin within sight of land and continue unbroken for hundreds of kilometers. No, this was definitely the wrong time of year to think about putting out to sea.

There was one exception, but it was an ominous one. A large Lucifan freighter traveling on methane steam and sails put into Mur-es-Werd in poor condition. It had been at sea for two years but hadn't been damaged by storms. It had been shelled by a ship the likes of which they'd never seen, which raced across the water on huge feet. The strange ship had no sails, gave off no steam, and yet had easily averaged ninety to a hundred kilometers an hour. Some speculated it wasn't a boat but a crustacean from the Pale Seas farther north than anyone had traveled. The trio heard of it in pubs and restaurants. Soon it was a common story much enlarged upon.

The story changed the atmosphere around the ports radically. But Bar-Woten maintained something else was up — a simple tale of strange doings at sea couldn't account for the way Mur-es-Werd was behaving. Kiril sensed it too. "Everyone's jumpy," he said. The Ibisian nodded.

The next day brought a warm, dry wind from the southwest. The skies were the color of bloody milk. Though the wind on the ground was mild, high above it tortured and twisted the clouds into thin, smooth ribbons and shot them with desert dirt. Mur-es-Werd was covered by a pink pall, and everyone walked warily as in a dangerous dream.

By evening it was clear and the winds died down. But the city was restless that night. The bars stayed open later than was normally allowed by law. Gangs of drunken men were herded home angrily in the early morning by women wielding cane brooms. The women wore dark dresses with strips of white tied around their arms. From a distance doves seemed to flutter around the men, driving them along the street with angry swishes.

Bar-Woten sat on the sand with his legs curled beneath him, watching and listening to the foamy waves. He thought they could tell him something. But they glowed and tossed and fussed incoherently, less powerfully than usual. Suddenly, they slowed to an oily trickle, rushing along the shore with a drawing bead of light. His neck hair prickled, and he

75

sat up on his knees wanting to run. It was near dawn — soon the sky would turn green at the zenith as it always had.

But ten minutes passed and the dark remained. Two fire doves twinkled pink and orange just above the northern horizon. A third, bluish in color, hovered above the western mountains.

They winked out.

Thousands in the city were awake, watching the sky with him. A low moan rose from the city, the sound of distant screams and wailing. Barthel and Kiril awoke abruptly and asked what was happening. Bar-Woten couldn't answer. How could anyone describe something they had never seen before?

The blackness of the sky turned muddy. Not a single fire dove was to be seen. Like the opening of two palms clasped together, the muddiness drew aside, and a vortex of dim purple, barely visible, spread across the sky, leaving another sort of darkness at its center.

This wasn't the warmly immediate, empty black that had always meant night for Hegira. It was a velvety dark strewn with glowing ribbons, and between and around and in these, twinkled points of light so fine no shape could be discerned. Clouds of light filled the sky. For the first time in memory of anyone living, starshine visibly brightened the land.

The city was silent under the frosty gaze of the stars. Barthel made a growling sound deep in his throat, and tears streamed down his cheeks. "Holy Allah," he said. "Blessed Allah."

Kiril's hand tightened around his belt. He felt like rolling in the sand and screaming.

The streets were soon crowded with crying, stumbling mobs. They washed onto the beaches and human waves met the water waves, forming a splashing tumult as the citizens

76

of Mur-es-Werd tried to put out the mad fevers that caused them to see such visions.

The stars were crossed by sudden, silky ripples. Kiril's stomach sank. He felt his body crawling this way and that, yet he wasn't moving; his muscles weren't twitching. His head threatened to turn inside out, but painlessly — a dreamy sort of dizziness, disorientation. The ocean waves grew brighter, became almost turquoise. He heard a deep bass note like the buzzing of giant bees. If the whole world had been a tapestry and somebody had started flapping it to shake out the dust, perhaps this was how it would feel — he didn't know. For a time he thought he would be better off dead.

The rippling in the sky stopped, and the stars steadied. The beach was encased in silence. The people around them moved slowly; even falling they drifted like puffs of down.

Looking up, Bar-Woten thought he was going to black out. At the periphery of his eye he could see darkness close in, cutting out the stars. But the dizziness was gone, and his head seemed all right. The stars were being obscured again. At the edge of the closing circle the points of light became lines of purple, twisted, and winked out. The familiar empty black returned. One by one, flickering, the fire doves resumed their glows. The sky at zenith turned green, then purple, then bronze; the dawn was picking up where it had left off.

The display had taken about five minutes. Everyone stood in silence for perhaps five minutes more, then looked at each other, embarrassed, and returned to their homes, trying to act as if everything was normal.

But Bar-Woten knew nothing would ever be normal again. He smiled crookedly. Then he began to laugh.

Ten

Barthel left the beach alone before midday and took a twisting road up the city's central hill. For a few hundred meters he walked alongside a crumbling wall centuries old. Grass grew in the chinks between stones. It had become part of the ground now, like the shell of a dead snail. The wall no longer served as armor but as a place for people to walk by and things to grown in. From the top of the Kassarva, the fortress that circled the summit, he could look down across the town and port and think with nothing to bother him. Insects buzzed hypnotically through the dried grass and sparse flowers. A large temple was visible through the trees far below, ceramic domes glinting at each of its five corners. Inside it, too, looked like a fortress. There was a courtyard and small buildings within the courtyard arranged in a *tomoye*. Birds flew above the temple — gulls, curlews, and others he hadn't learned the names of. Some resembled hawks but caught fish by the sea and had red and white feathers in their crests.

He felt singularly ugly and afraid. The predawn unveiling had struck him deeply. What had it told him, that message for all to see? He didn't know. But it made him feel as tiny as the ants beneath him, carrying bits of white stuff in a line under his legs into a hole a few yards away. All these creatures — ants, birds, builders of temples — had been put here by the blessed One, Who had unveiled the sky that morning.

"I am Barthel," he told the sky with tears in his eyes. "I am small. Did you do all these things that I might see them, smell them? I've done nothing in return for you, Allah. I haven't even learned from them." He asked what it was Allah wanted him to do, and Allah told him this: Survive. He nodded. He would survive. The Bey had taught him how to survive. What else then? Father and mother and family.

That was all the voice said. Be to them what they would have wished you to be.

His lips curled. He stood up from the grass and gravel and brushed his ragged pants off. "I'll also find out where your light comes from," he said. "You'll be happy to see I'm clever enough to figure that out."

Bar-Woten wandered through the closed and confused streets. Kiril followed half-heartedly, not wanting to be left alone on the beach. No shops were open, and the people who passed them were solemn and tired. The city was quiet.

"What was it?" Kiril asked after a long silence. "Have you ever seen anything like it where you've been?"

"No," Bar-Woten answered. "The sky is the same wherever you go. What we saw last night was seen everywhere, even on the other side of Hegira."

"Then what was it?"

"You tell me."

"Stars, of course. But the Second-born have no stars over their heads. That's the way it's always been."

"Do we have stars over our heads now?"

"Not that we see. But something must stop us from seeing them — a lid, a hatch. And God opened that lid last night to show us glory."

"He showed us stars. Glory is what you feel when looking at them. Myself, I felt the glory perhaps. But more important, I learned that we are not so different

79

from the First-born. We are not cursed. It may be — "
But Bar-Woten stopped and shook his head.

"It was beautiful," Kiril said reverently, walking beside
the Ibisian. He almost felt affection for the older warrior, as
if they shared something no others did: their inner thoughts
on an unprecedented act of God.

"It made my heart icy. It looked young out there."

"What do you mean?" Kiril asked.

"It wasn't all stars," he said. "There were a lot of other
things out there. The fog. Maybe we didn't see a starry sky
at all. Maybe we saw something else that we haven't read
about yet."

They found Barthel wandering by the wharves, where all
the moored boats knocked idle and empty against the pier
buffers. They rejoined silently and walked along the lengthy
quays, smelling the sea — which smelled no differently —
and listening to the cat-cries of the seabirds. The birds
sounded the same.

A five-masted steamer had docked at the end of a pier,
three stacks poking jauntily above the steel hull. Gangs of
sailors and stevedores hauled cargo from the holds amidships
and scurried down planks, to a warehouse at the side of the
pier. Cranes and winches lifted the heavier crates onto
dollies. It was the only ship so occupied, and it wasn't
Lucifan. They had never seen its flag before nor heard the
tongue the men were speaking. Bar-Woten motioned for
them to follow. They boarded unnoticed, or ignored, and
watched the proceedings with interest.

Bar-Woten spotted a man who stood out from the clamor,
walking with deliberate speed along the dock to the gangway.
Khaki pantaloons ballooned from his legs, and he wore a
tight blue waistcoat over a white linen shirt. He boarded as
if he were long familiar with the swaying rope bridge and
made his way to the forecastle, striding past the three where

they leaned on the starboard railing. Bar-Woten stepped forward and addressed him in Lucifan.

"I'm busy," the man said. "What're you bothering me for?"

"We're looking for work and passage."

"Talk later." He hurried off. The Ibisian raised his eyebrow and winked at his companions. That was some sort of encouragement — not an offhand dismissal.

They inspected the ship in the meanwhile. Kiril counted their monies speculatively. "Look, with the cash from selling the horses — that and what we've earned — we can last four, five more days. Not much time."

"I know nothing about ships," Bar-Woten said, making it seem of small importance to his judgment. "Nor I," Barthel concurred hopefully.

"We'll have to eat. I'm tired of a sandy bed. Tired of carrying everything I own on my back."

"We've got a long way to go, friend. There'll be a lot more of that ahead."

"We should take any chance we get to board a ship, though," Kiril pursued. Barthel looked at him with dismay.

"No argument," Bar-Woten said. "What do you think we've been planning? You're the one who's been reluctant."

"I, too," Barthel said. "The sea is an unpleasant bed, Bey."

"But I mean to say that I'd rather go to sea than live a vagrant."

"You're inconsistent. You were a vagrant on your pilgrimage. I found you in an alley. You have a sudden taste for comfort?"

"Then let's not discuss it," Kiril said, growing angry.

"Certainly."

They waited until late afternoon. By then, the ship was

unloaded, and the sailors and dockworkers had gone to ship's mess and homes on the land, respectively.

"The captain will take a walk after his meal," Bar-Woten predicted. "We'll talk to him again when he does."

The man reappeared just before dusk. The deck was deserted except for the three and a sailor standing watch on the stern. The captain walked over and looked at them sharply. "You want passage?" he asked. They nodded. "What ships have you sailed on?"

"None," Bar-Woten said.

"You think this is University of the Sea, eh?"

"I think we can learn fast enough not to stumble."

"You been to sea before, for a long time? A year or two?"

The Ibisian shook his head.

"Then what can I use you for? Mops? Who told you I needed hands?"

No one did.

"Then what makes you think I do?"

They weren't sure he did.

"Dammit, I have to take my stock where I can! Don't think that I like your faces because I say yes. Take it that the sky spoke and no one wants to sign on! They all believe the seas will swallow them when the world ends."

"It's not going to end," Bar-Woten said.

"Of course not. But sailors are bastards for a pretty story of *ginnunga-gaps*," the captain said. "You'll report to the quartermaster tomorrow morning. We sail with the second bell. I am Captain Prekari. Conditions are board and thirty standard thalers a month, your positions and rank to be determined according to merit and ability. Accepted?"

They nodded. The captain looked them over again and marched off muttering. Kiril turned around and looked into the filthy water lapping against the ship's side.

"Where do we spend the night?" he asked.

"On the beach. Say farewell to your sand fleas."

Eleven

The ship was called *Trident* and came from a land just south of the Pale Seas. Her crew was a quiet, strong breed with few quarrels and steady loyalty. Such emotions sustained a ship over the distances she had to travel — discontent could only sink her.

Bar-Woten studiously set to learning the language they spoke, which to Kiril sounded Germanic. He had never spent much time learning the Germanic texts of the Obelisk — so far as the Mediwevans had read, they consisted of incomprehensible treatises on mechanics and a few scattered fairy tales mixed with heavy philosophy — but he knew enough to get along. Barthel had a harder time.

The *Trident* took her cargo of fiber, dried fish, and machine parts aboard a day after the three reported to the quartermaster. By the next morning they were at sea. They traveled along the coast eastward for several days, passing four inlets surrounded by cliffs several kilometers tall. Huge birds nested there, the sailors told them — albatrosses with webbed feet that could match a man's arm span. The exaggeration wasn't enough to make Bar-Woten think they were lying. Besides, now and then dark flying shapes could actually be seen, and at that distance they had to be impressively large to be spotted at all. No one lived in the fjords. Few people ever went there.

At a port called Trincoma they put off a cargo of dried fish and copra and took aboard more hemp as well as a number of unlabeled boxes. Kiril thought they might be drugs — Bar-Woten thought otherwise. "Spices," he ventured. "Did you smell the crates?" Barthel confirmed the Bey's guess by announcing they smelled like saffron — and there were several tons of it aboard.

The dark inhabitants of Mur-es-Werd had given way in Trincoma to light brown peoples with broad noses, thick lips, tall, noble foreheads and eyes white as bone. Kiril compared his own pale skin and regular features and found himself wanting. Each day he grew more dissatisfied with himself. But he was learning the duties of a sailor rapidly enough and received few complaints.

They began their first push far from land by the end of the week. On Skeitag, the day after Geistag and the day before Duvetag in the language of the *Trident*'s crew, the ship set her sails and brought her boilers to full steam. Her triple screws churned the water below the iron stern until she was outracing the gentle wind. Sails were pulled in, and Kiril was taught the art of maintaining the methane supply in the ship.

Tanks were kept on each side of the forecastle deck that gathered rainwater when possible or served as storage for seawater desalinated by the sun in plastic tarp-slings rigged between the masts. Into this water were placed quantities of dried seaweed and dormant infusion. The tanks were capped, and man-operated pumps began to collect and store the resulting gases in a few days. The stink that sometimes escaped was regrettable — but it kept the boilers going when the wind was low and provided electricity at all times. Small chugging cylinders operated two generators for the ship's current.

Bar-Woten took instruction in ship's mechanics. He enjoyed the challenge of the engines more than he thought he would — more than he let on he did — and soon was apprenticed to the boiler-tender and his thirty helpers.

Barthel, least literate of the three as far as the Teutans were concerned, was given standard mast-monkey duties and was contented with such exertions. Though he frequently had to crawl out on a yardarm over open, churning water, his fear of the sea diminished to a healthy respect. His skin became even more bronzed. His muscles developed into flexible and agile bulges, which he thought he might put to good advantage in other places besides the rigging. The crew of the *Trident* was integrated, male and female.

Kiril sighed at this eventuality and resigned himself to quiet regret. Bar-Woten began his inevitable romancing. For the first few weeks, however, the voyage went smoothly enough.

The work of the day was over for their watches when Kiril and Bar-Woten met on the quarterdeck to talk and relax before the evening meal. The ship would soon be midway between Obelisks, where the ocean air would be cooler and the weather less predictable. Thus far the *Trident* had avoided the seasonal storms that plagued parts of the coast south of them. They talked about rough storms and what they must be like as they leaned over the brass railings, looking into the water. The hazy horizon was interrupted by shadows of distant coastline.

"I sometimes think we'll forget what we're really after," Kiril said. "Or you will, at least. It isn't as immediate a goal for you."

"It's a goal," Bar-Woten said. "No need to worry about that."

"I can't even remember her face," Kiril admitted. His throat caught suddenly. "I hardly remember what it was like to hold her."

"Then tell me about her. Maybe that will help."

But Kiril found words difficult, especially before the burly Ibisian. "She was at least as tall as Barthel, perhaps a centimeter or two taller," he began. "Blonde hair as long as her waist when it wasn't tied in a bun, with a tail down to her shoulder blades. She had . . . has a soft voice. Can I still say she has?"

"I don't know," Bar-Woten said.

"Small feet. She seems so far away now. I'm not even sure I'm the same man who loved her."

"Men have gone off on more foolish journeys for less certain reasons."

"You know, hm?" Kiril said, not intending to gibe.

Bar-Woten didn't take offense. "I know," he agreed. "What was her family like?"

"They didn't like me much. I suppose no family likes a suitor — they bring too many changes. But I didn't fit in with their activities. She never accused me of that, or minded, but her family was very clannish, played games and sports together all the time — she had a huge family, twelve brothers and sisters. Her father was a quiet man. He managed a business in a small town called Torres de Cristobal. He owned a small ranch and raised cattle. I was a scrittori — not a very reliable occupation, not much better than being a student or a theologian. But I was doing well enough that they couldn't fault me my choice of lifetimes."

"Choice of lifetimes?"

"Of course. A man chooses when he is to be born, to carry out a certain task on Hegira. If he chooses wrongly, then he comes at an inopportune time, and he can only turn out bad or useless. I was doing well enough not to be useless."

"What was her name?" Bar-Woten asked.

"Elena," he said.

Barthel began taking lessons in navigation from three deck

officers. He was getting better with the language, and two of his teachers could speak passable Lucifan. In turn for his lessons he offered them lessons in Arbuck, which some of the western coastal countries spoke and which had always been a mystery to the crew of the *Trident*.

Navigation on Hegira, they explained, was entirely different from navigation as described by the Obelisk texts. There were different objects to be sighted and different problems to be dealt with. The meteorology of Hegira was radically different from old Earth, and there were no stars or sun or moon to use as guides. Instead the paths of certain fire doves were charted, and each fire dove was given a name according to its peculiar qualities. In all there were at least five hundred different fire doves, two dozen of which were easily discernible. They could be identified by color and brightness, not unlike the methods used by the First-born to distinguish stars, but the fire doves were obviously not stars. They were not fixed — they wandered in relation to each other according to complex orbits, all of which appeared to be centered on Hegira. Not all the orbits had been calculated, however. Only ten especially bright fire doves were used for most navigational problems.

One of the major problems of navigation was knowing when a fire dove would be illuminated. Each had its own cycle of light and dark, which ranged from seven hours to six months. It was considered bad form to be tracking a fire dove and have it unexpectedly go out on you.

During the day prevailing winds — which seldom shifted — were used to indicate direction, according to how the ship ran with them. Some ocean currents were also used as guides. When weather permitted, the Obelisks were referred to, and these fixed points were the most reliable. The four points of the compass weren't used in their normal sense by Hegirans. Magnetized needles didn't point any particular direction, though it was rumored that lodestone poles did exist to the very far northwest. The side of an Obelisk that began with the invocation text was called the north side. Left of it was west, right east, and opposite, south. Beyond that one traveled by original orientation, using Obelisks and fire doves as references.

The *Trident* would soon lose sight of the Obelisk Tara in Mediweva, and of the Obelisk Onmassee east of it in the central highlands of Fedderland. Trincoma was the westernmost port of Fedderland, and while the Obelisk Onmassee was not visible from that city, a kilometer out to sea brought it into plain view.

Barthel studied the books and charts given to him. They obviously did not come from Obelisk texts. Therefore the crew of the *Trident*, though they came from a land that had access to an Obelisk, didn't share the prejudices of the Mediwevans. He read voraciously.

One of his teachers was a deck officer named Avra, a woman at least twice Bar-Woten's age, with thick black hair and a thin, stern face. Her eyes were the same green as the phantom lights that formed rings in the waves at night. She spoke in a small, precise voice and carried her shoulders with an arrogant squareness belying her personality, which was pleasant and gracious. She was a widow. Her husband had been a methane-tender, and they had sailed on the *Trident* for twenty years together in more foreign ports and strange seas than anyone else aboard, even the captain, who had joined the ship four years before. At age fifteen she had hired on as a cook, and all her training and schooling had been aboard the *Trident*. She was an excellent teacher, and she found the Khemite an eager pupil.

Bar-Woten remained quietly puzzled by the *Trident*. She had no true home port, though most of her crew called the country of Weggismarche home. They were heading there now, by way of a few ports along the Bicht av Genevar, a broad archipelago between Weggismarche and the Obelisk Daana. In a few months they would pass the Ocean Obelisk. The *Trident* had spent most of her half-century in these waters plying trade between the islands and Weggismarche. In this way she had developed a good reputation that sustained her when she had been isolated from her previous owners through several revolutions in Weggismarche. For a few harsh years she had become a pirate of sorts.

But that was all past now. The *Trident* carried only a token complement of guns that were powerful enough for defense, but would never let her play the role of a raiding ship. Besides, she wasn't fast enough.

What puzzled the Ibisian was the spirit of cooperation that powered the ship almost as much as the wind. Survival in the tough trade of the Bicht av Genevar and elsewhere was apparently determined by blatant and dependable honesty. He had never known a system run in such a way. He doubted its efficacy.

Kiril accepted it with a joyous heart. He listened intently to stories told by the crew of dozens of encounters with civilizations that had never known foreign trade, or even foreigners — without a single mishap. "She's a goddess!" he told Bar-Woten enthusiastically, patting the varnished oak railings. "One king even called her a *Kwan-Yin* — Mercy. What a ship we chose to join!"

The Ibisian kept his silence and learned all he could about the lands the *Trident* had visited. He kept a notebook in which he drew his maps and charts and recorded private observations.

They had been at sea for three months without sight of land, navigating by the Ten Agreeable Fire Doves, when a call for general quarters was rung. The crew took positions in a few minutes. Nothing could be spotted from the decks, but the lookout in the mainmast tower-nest had spotted something odd ahead of them. Within a quarter hour people on the decks spotted it too.

Kiril was standing next to a wiry old man who usually supervises repairs to the ship's sails and deck canvas. The old sailor's eyes were sharper than Kiril's — he held his hand above them and mumbled something about it being the largest he'd ever seen.

"What is it?" Kiril asked, almost shaking. The sea was suddenly a very unpleasant place again, green and cold and unknown.

"*Untersay draken*," the canvasmaker answered.

"What's that?" Kiril wanted — and at the same time didn't want — specifics.

"*Spruten.*"

"I don't know that word."

"*Ochobras, diesbras, dolfijn-manker.*"

No better off than before, he turned his eyes back to the horizon and saw it. At first it looked like a thick tangle of what the sailors called sargass, a weed that formed in ocean eddies like floating islands. But its pulpy tendrils took on a ropey sort of life which made his neck hairs crawl. Sometimes it was pink, sometimes blue. He regretted ever leaving his landlocked home.

"*Polypus*," another sailor said, approaching the rail to get a better view, pointing with a lean brown finger. Kiril looked at him, and the man raised his shaggy eyebrows urging him to see it while he could. "Rare sight!" he explained. "Makes a seaman of you."

"Or a pudding," another said. A few women and one young girl joined the group, and Kiril tried to pull himself together for their benefit. But he still trembled.

The *polypus* — a word close enough to the Mediwevan equivalent that he could understand they were talking about a squid — was basking without much concern off the port side, barely a hundred meters away. The *Trident* was giving it a wide berth. It was common knowledge that *untersay drakens*, like fishermen's floats, carried nine tenths of their bulk below the water line.

At night the sea was alive with growing lights. This was truly the realm of *drakens*, Kiril learned — a hundred leagues of squid and glowing fish and *fliegen-say-drakens*, which could land on deck and squash a man, but were harmless otherwise. Then there was the possibility of meeting a pack of true serpents, not shy like the squid, not harmless like the flying beasts, but carnivorous and nasty and difficult to drive off.

Bar-Woten was unpleasantly awed as he stared over the railing and saw the lights pass and flash in the depths. Overhead were the fire doves in the velvet black sky, and below that the glowing soup of the sea's surface, and beneath that luminous spots like eyes as wide across as the spread of his arms. The night was alive with seeing things and glowing things and curious unknown things. He had never known discomfort — or even fear — like what he felt now, even on the worst and most wretched nights of the March.

But with morning the sea was blue and bright and the air was warmer. No more fleshy masses were spotted, and some cheer returned.

Barthel watched the temperature rise on the ship's thermometers as they entered the region of the Ocean Obelisk. He frowned each time he stood at the base of the mainmast, where the instruments were mounted on a mahogany plaque. He scratched his head and squinted comically. Then, when the Obelisk was in plain view, just before nightfall as the sky dimmed and turned gold and green, his frown cleared. He looked at the thermometers with astonishment and started to shout.

"It's simple!" he yelled. "It's so beautifully simple!"

Twelve

Bar-Woten and Kiril took turns leaning on the wrench, grunting and straining in the close dark heat of the engine room bilge. The wrench was wrapped around a fist-sized nut that held a tension plate in position, keeping a secondary rod on the high-pressure cylinder in line with its swing alley. It had been rubbing for a day, causing a hideous screech with each pump and swing that echoed through the engine and made the crankshaft tremble and buck. With the gradual loosening of the nut the tension plate could be shifted by deft hammer blows until the cylinder rod crept back into line. It was rough, filthy work with old paint rubbing off on their pants and sweat flooding over their cotton brow-bands and prickling in their eyes. They set the wrench and hammer down for a rest. Bar-Woten rubbed the blisters on his hand.

Feet banged down the ladder from the upper engine room catwalk. "I've figured it out!" Barthel shouted. "I've got it!"

He sat down next to them on one of the main bearings, squirming on the uneven surface, and told them. It came out in a quick and happy babble, in Mediwevan, which most of the attending engine hands didn't understand, leaving them to sit and listen blankly on the port stringer beam and bilge keelson.

"That means the Obelisks have light and heat on top," he concluded. "That explains why some deep canyons are dark the same way all the time and others aren't."

Bar-Woten nodded, too tired to think. Kiril leaned against a condenser pipe and said it sounded convincing.

"It's very important," Barthel said, disappointed that his excitement wasn't communicating itself. He looked from face to face and tried to explain it to the other sailors in broken Teutan. They nodded agreeably. Frustrated, he stood and brushed his pants off, turned around, and looked at the engine as though he distrusted it and all other deaf and dumb things he couldn't explain himself to. He climbed out of the engine-well and went about on deck to look for Avra.

Kiril and Bar-Woten switched with another pair of sailors, and the wrenching and hammering continued.

The water became warmer and more turbulent. Great spouts tore the sea into ragged shards to the west. In a few days the water cooled slightly, but the temperature increased the closer they approached the Ocean Obelisk.

Avra helped Barthel put his theory into writing, and together they gathered facts and figures to back it up. He was disappointed to find the idea wasn't original with him, but he still worked to prove his assertions, and Avra tutored him on how to go about the research.

The Ocean Obelisk passed on the port side the day after the engine overhaul was completed. Kiril watched it from the railing and thought about Barthel's theory, wondering how correct he was. His world was taking shape more each day. He thought he might have it all in the palm of his hand in a few more years. The Obelisks were higher than the air, and the sun did not rise or set on the Second-born, but grew bright or dim, and perhaps hid where nothing but its light could be seen . . . He daydreamed for an instant, and the Obelisk turned scaly and writhed like the tail of a dragon. He shook his head briskly to clear it. In a week the Obelisk was in the horizon haze.

The smell of the sea changed as they approached the

waters of the Bicht. Islands grew more numerous, some with small fishing settlements and huts on tall poles. The sea frequently rose above the islands during a storm, Bar-Woten learned. It was a rough life. Still people clung like barnacles, and he knew the glue that held them was the past. Where the past had meaning, people stayed.

The *Trident* did brisk trade between the islands, also acting as a hauler and mediator. Her principal load was destined for Weggismarche, but she had several tons of tools and nets which she'd picked up on other landfalls. Kiril and Barthel helped with the inventory. Bar-Woten drove one of the motor launches that delivered the goods to the islands lacking port facilities.

In these weeks they saw white beaches backed with palm trees that rustled and crackled in the breeze, and high green mountains thick with brush no man had ever crawled through, and islands so big there was no way to tell they weren't the mainland until you had sailed completely around one and seen the same banyan tree from two directions. Kiril breathed it in and blew it out and took energy from it all. At night he ran his hands along his back and felt the ridges of lash scars there, asking: Who did this? I did? Not I. The other one.

The Young One.

He worked with the loading crews on cargo watches until sweat covered him in a fine sheen. He helped trim and refit piping from the methane tanks and went with the boats to kelp beds to gather the great underwater trees. On deck they hung in canvas-covered bags until they were cut and stacked to dry. The smell was outrageous. In a few days, though, they were in neat odorless blocks, boxed and stored for use in the methane-generation tanks. The wind was from the sea, and the kelp was from the sea, and he knew, as he sweated in the day and felt his scars by night, that the

Trident did nothing to the sea that any other sea creature didn't do. He was no longer a penitent, a traveler out of fear, but a crewman of the *Trident*.

Conversely, Bar-Woten enjoyed the work and grew familiar with the sea, but was not part of the ship. He could never wholeheartedly join anything again. He worked with the boilers and the engine and knew them for what they were, pieces of metal that filled and pumped and thrust, not parts of a living thing.

Barthel's enthusiasm seldom reached him. Most of what the Khemite was learning from Avra wouldn't be much use to them when they landed in the north and started the trek again. It seemed to Bar-Woten that the original journey was losing steam. It was being absorbed into this lesser, niggling trip across sea and between islands.

The central island of the Bicht was called Golumbine. It was twenty-five hundred kilometers from Weggismarche. On extremely clear days, the Weggismarche Obelisk could be seen from its northern side as an almost invisible line. The *Trident* sailed around the eastern tip, passing huge pillars of granite topped with temples carved from solid rock thousands of years ago. Above the beaches, in the craggy hills, three statues rose from the jungle. Each was a hundred meters tall, made from bronze almost black with the centuries. The central sculpture was a woman dancing, her right leg crooked to put her foot just over her left knee, both arms held out with palms up toward the sky. She was rounded and stocky, built to hold her weight as much as to resemble a woman. Her hair radiated in bronze sunbursts, a fan of metal twenty meters wide. To each side her companion statues were serpents curling around central columns of rock white as snow, except where the bronze had stained them green.

The *Trident* put into the deepwater port in the north of the island eight months after leaving Mur-es-Werd, and the brown, light-haired inhabitants welcomed them to Golumbine. Liberty was granted to all aboard the ship but a skeleton watch, of which Bar-Woten was a disgruntled member.

That evening the crew of the *Trident* feasted in a palace made of quartz. It was only the climax of a heady day spent as near-heroes, welcomed after a long absence at sea by a kingdom the *Trident* had saved from starvation during droughts three years before. The crew and officers were led along the bund in the late afternoon after the day's business had been completed. They were seated in a shady building of white wood slats and rattan roofing. While they were served drinks in the hard rinds of *sati*, a juicy red-fleshed fruit, wagons pulled by large island deer parked in front. They climbed in with drinks in hand and were driven along a path that snaked through an orchard, rose gently to a hilltop, and after an exhilarating downhill gallop, presented them to the stone city of Mappu.

Mappu was at least ten thousand years old, Avra told Kiril and Barthel as they rode in the cart. A thousand years ago it had been rebuilt because its stones had grown too worn to be dignified. In all that time it had known only three dynasties of royal families. Each had succeeded without bloodshed under the decrees of the priests and priestesses of Dat, the goddess whose statue rose on the island's eastern peninsula. There had been some war with western islands during the past two hundred years, but Golumbine was now at peace. Its hundred-and-fifty-kilometer length supported fifty thousand people comfortably.

She finished her history just as the carts pulled up to the crystalline palace. The officers and crew stepped down and milled at the base of the white marble steps. Footprints had worn grooves in the stone. Above the steps a half-circle arch of white quartz led to the alcove of the main hall. The arch was covered with etched figurines engaged in every aspect of living — farming, herding, studying, building, eating, making love, giving birth, dying . . . coronation and funerals, life and death in dizzying detail. Barthel patiently ignored them. Kiril was less circumspect. He walked with the others into the alcove beneath the arch, frustrated and curious to examine it longer. They were taken into the main hall.

Curtains and banners hung rippling with red and green ribbons tied at their ends, suspended from rafters of dark rich wood inlaid with bone and ivory friezes. Low tables covered by white cloth with a bowl at each place setting awaited them, covering the floor of the hall. The men and women and children of the *Trident* took their seats on pillows. The captain was given a seat of honor next to a simple wooden throne.

At one side of the hall was a curtained stage. The curtains coursed with the activity behind them, sequins twinkling in the red and green and blue silk.

Everyone stood. Whispers passed — the Queen and King were approaching. Kiril expected long, fine robes and blaring trumpets, but there was no fanfare or pomp. He could barely see the throne over the heads of his crewmates, but what he did see caught him off guard.

The Queen and King were little more than a meter high, well proportioned and graying with age, dressed in simple gray suits and lacking crowns or any overt signs of distinction. They took their seats — the Queen on her throne, the King at her feet. The meal was served.

The first course was clear broth soup with bits of crunchy vegetables floating in it, spiced with curry. Then came a dish of wheat grains steamed and topped with a sauce of shellfish and green beans. The main course was *matu paka*, beef and pork cooked in broth and butter and garnished with thick leaves of sweet cabbage. Barthel picked at it without enthusiasm — pork was a forbidden item for him — but Kiril thought he'd never tasted anything so delicious. A grain liqueur, sweet and biting, was served with thick cream and a coffeelike brew. Dessert followed. When the company was through with the spiced fruit and cream-egg chiffon, the entertainment began.

The curtains drew aside, showing a stage empty except for voluminous folds of blue cloth draped over hidden set pieces and lighted by dozens of insect-wax lamps. A single man dressed in blue rose from behind a draped box and stood on top of it, drawing a fan from his shirt and spreading it wide. He smiled, whistled, and beckoned with the fan to the left of the stage.

Some of the crew knew what to expect. Many others didn't, and a cry of dismay went up as the beast stalked onto the stage. Barthel felt a chill, as though he was seeing something ungodly.

It was about two meters tall and stood on thick, powerful hind legs, balanced by a sinuous tail. It was sky blue around its throat and stomach and dewlaps and enamel green like a beetle everywhere else. Its eyes were red as rubies and ringed with black and orange. It was a magnificent animal, its gait as smooth as a dancer's, its long mouth studded with glittering teeth. It bowed to the man in blue and hunkered down in the middle of the stage with its tail curled under it. It bird-blinked back to front with nictitating membranes as it surveyed the audience. A thick black tongue slithered between iridescent lips.

A woman dressed in red baggy pants and shirt stood up and climbed onto another draped pedestal. She produced a second fan, spread it, and beckoned to the right. A man-tall, heavy-beaked bird crossed the stage and perched in front of her, beak open, staring and twisting its head. It looked more alarmed than its reptile companion. A second man summoned two lions, and a second woman brought out a tiger four meters long from head to tail with gray-green and white stripes instead of the usual black and orange. The animals took their positions quietly.

The first man began a gliding dance around the stage between the animals. The tiger licked one paw contentedly. The bird stalked forward and joined the man in a strange, appealing ballet. The first woman began her own dance, and the tiger stalked with perfect precision under her swirling legs. The reptile stood up.

With the lions joining in, they became a shifting in-and-out sequence of fluid bodies and startling colors. The first dance ended with one woman riding the tiger and a man leading the reptile by a short halter. Kiril couldn't break his eyes away. He expected disaster and carnivorous reprisal at any instant. As the curtains closed the crew of the *Trident* crossed their arms and slapped their palms against their biceps. Kiril and Barthel mimicked the applause. A grin covered the Khemite's face, and his eyes sparkled like a child's.

The chandeliers lighting the hall tinkled and quivered slightly. Kiril felt his neck hair prickling. A low, inaudible vibration passed through the floor and tables. The hall was suddenly quiet. Behind the curtains the sounds of scuffling and growls interrupted the silence.

There were no quakes on Hegira. There were no records of quakes except on the Obelisks; it was assumed they were plagues visited upon the First-born in moments of hubris. But very clearly the palace lights were swaying, and the floor sustained its subsensuous murmur. The King and Queen stood up hesitantly, and a retinue of guards surrounded them. A man dressed in flowing, shiny green robes passed along one side of the hall with two lackeys in red following, each carrying bowls of incense. They left the hall.

The reptile poked through the curtains and stood on the

apron of the stage, uncertain and unwilling to jump into the audience. A trainer dressed in black came out and led it backstage again. Its tail swished back and forth like a cat's under the curtain.

Barthel crouched wide-eyed by the table.

The captain ordered his crew to be seated.

Outside, it had been dark for an hour and a slight drizzle was falling. The watch on the *Trident* felt the tremor as a singing in the hull. Water rippled from the shore, and the logs of the bund creaked.

Bar-Woten walked up the ladder from the engine room and went to the port side to stare out into the dark. He could see nothing but the patient gleam of the fire doves and small, fitful glows of disturbed animals in the water. He squinted his eyes, looking directly north.

A hand span up from the horizon, something dimly flickered, and it wasn't a fire dove. It was in the same vicinity as the Weggismarche Obelisk — could, in fact, have been the top of the spire — and it suggested heat lightning on a warm summer night. Its flicker sent sympathetic flashes across the sky like messages between gods.

Suddenly, from across the sea, it was daylight. To the south the glow was dull gray and listless, but in the north the day was full and bright. Bar-Woten saw the Obelisk clearly, a line of white drawn from the sky down, its top lost in the sheet of daylight glow.

It was no longer vertical. With clocklike slowness it changed its angle. The tremble that made his feet ache and his head throb was a much-reduced and distant effect. The Obelisk was tilting and falling.

He was enough of a seaman now and had studied the charts enough to know that the fall of anything of such size would create havoc along that distant sea and coastline. The result would be more quakes, and something he had never imagined until now, but knew was inevitable.

The sea would rise from the collision of world and spire like an unleashed monster. He knew instinctively it would carry itself to Golumbine and beyond. He had no idea how fast such a vibration could travel through water or the land beneath, but it would be rapid.

He ran to the poop deck and told a cabin boy to take a message to the captain. As the boy ran to the gangway and crossed to the shore, the Ibisian saw the final moment of the fall.

In awful silence the spire dropped below the horizon. The daylight flickered and blinked out.

With agonizing awareness of his ignorance, Bar-Woten tried to calculate how long they had. He had learned enough about basic physics in the last few months to make a guess — it would be measured in hours instead of minutes — but how many? Sound traveled through rock faster than through air or water.

In a half hour the crew and hundreds of Golumbines were running along the bund and docks.

The captain boarded without ceremony and issued a call to general quarters. "We're taking the ship out to sea," he shouted. Sails were rigged and steam was brought up. The boilers protested the rapid heating by creaking and pounding.

In another half hour the ship was ready to cruise at one third out of the harbor. The Golumbines followed its example, hauling their boats ashore if they were small enough or following the *Trident* out to sea. Bar-Woten watched the barges and outrigged clippers following in their wake. In the wavering glow of lamps mounted along the sides of the boats, he saw the faces of sailors working at oars and rigging or simply waiting, eyes north and mouths wide.

When the engines were up to full steam he turned his deck gauge over to another sailor and went to find Kiril.

The Mediwevan was stowing gear with a dozen other men. Bar-Woten helped them, and as they worked he asked Kiril what he had read about big waves and the First-born.

"They were called tidal waves," Kiril said. "That's about all I know. But we don't have any tides here — I'm not even sure they were caused by tides on Earth." He shook his head. They'd never seen really big waves except those caused by a storm at sea, such as the waves on the beaches in Mures-Werd. "If the Obelisk fell — "

"It fell!" Bar-Woten said firmly.

"Then we probably won't survive."

"What are they going to do on the island?"

"Head for the highest hills they can find. Or behave as people usually do and be washed out to sea. I don't know! The captain warned them, but he doesn't know what he's talking about any more than the rest of us."

The *Trident* was four kilometers northwest of the island when the captain decided the water was deep enough. The sails were furled, and all the ship's hatches battened and bolted. The bow was swung about in the direction of the Obelisk, and the boilers cooled. The excess methane in the tanks and fire chamber was blown out the rear through valves. All compressed gas tanks were double sealed and anchored to the deck plates and beams with thick rubber-coated chains.

It was quiet. The crew secured themselves below decks to stanchions and bulkhead hooks, using slipknots in case they had to abandon ship. The *Trident* made her usual share of ship noises. The water lapped against her steel hull.

An hour and a half after the fall the distant island hummed and wailed like a bottled demon. The deck watch and the captain and officers on the bridge observed through binoculars. Trees cast off their leaves like dogs shivering water.

From the north they could hear a wind rising. It sounded like a moaning woman. In the dark, clouds began to build and obscure the fire doves along the horizon.

The ship's electrical system was shut off. Below decks, the crew lighted hand-held candles.

Above the *Trident*, the sky whipped itself into a glittering frosty green foam. Snow fell in hand-sized flakes onto the ship and the sea. The air chilled, then became as warm as a mid-summer night and thick with moisture. Water dribbled down the bulkheads.

Ahead, kilometers off, a mound of sea rose across the entire horizon.

"That's it," Prekari said.

The bow jumped and the ship screamed. Rivets popped along the deck like bullets. With the speed of a cargo boom hauling a light load, the wave brought the ship to its mammoth peak, bucked it about in white water and foam, and twisted it around. It lurched sideways into a trough like a toboggan down a slope of snow, veering and weaving, water pouring over its decks. The mizzenmast snapped free from the poop deck and toppled over, breaking lines and driving the spanker spar through the steel plates of the deck like an arrow. Barthel stared at the splintered shaft, barely a meter from where he was strapped down.

The dog-tail waves that followed bounced the *Trident* vigorously, but she took them with little trouble. In the wake of the big wave the water churned and boiled. Things rose from the sea bottom that had lain undisturbed for centuries. A barnacled and crumpled wreck bobbed to the surface almost under the *Trident*, masts and hull above water for several seconds before it sank like a stone. The sea was clouded and silty, and big gouts of bubbling mud exploded.

Tangled knots of seaweed floated like the hair of drowned women.

Aching and shaken, the crew untied themselves and scrambled on deck to see what could be done. They shook their heads in disbelief. Some cried — men, women, and children alike. People hugged each other like long lost friends.

"It's not over yet," Bar-Woten said. No one listened — they were wild with elation and danced on the deck as the air grew moist again. Snow drifted peacefully to the deck. A snapping cold wind raced over the ship and painted hoarfrost on the rigging.

The captain called from the bridge for all to brace. A second wave was coming, larger than the first.

They had only a few minutes to get below and tie themselves in again. The *Trident* took water in her bilges faster than the pumps could remove it and rode lower by a meter, listing slightly as she turned into the approaching mountain.

Kiril helped tie the last errant child and took hold of the edges of a beam, knowing he had no time to rope himself. His stomach seemed to fall to his feet. Outside was a sound none had ever heard before — the insane deafening roar of atoms being destroyed. A flash covered the sky.

The ship plunged. The bulkhead of an aft compartment separated and bent like the metal in a child's toy. Kiril swung around and lost his grip, bounced off a secured collection of crates, and fell somewhere, he didn't know where. It was dark at the bottom.

Thirteen

Golumbine was almost unrecognizable. The wharves and bunds were gone or covered with mud and silt. The long boathouses had been ground into wet and splintered wood, and the boats were scattered wreckage. The island lay quiet as a tomb. No one moved. The ship drifted into the filthy harbor, fragments of wood and corpses of animals and humans bumping against her bow. The city of Mappu was not visible from the ocean and may have been protected by its surround of hills, but they could see no activity at all. To a height of fifty meters the wooded hills were ragged and stripped.

Dat and one of her guardians still stood upright, though smeared with weed and mud to the waist. The other serpent column wasn't visible. The daylight was milky and incomplete, the north gray and dark.

Deathly tired, retching from the smell of corruption in the warm still air, the people of the *Trident* watched as their ship dropped anchor.

Bar-Woten came on deck, his face pale and lined with grease and dirt. Barthel stood by the railing on the main deck and stared listlessly at the island.

"He has some broken ribs," the Ibisian said. Barthel nodded. "Something may be wrong with his head too. The doctor doesn't know for sure."

There was no tide to scour the beaches or take the flotsam out to sea. Only a mild seaward current flowed through the harbor. In a few more days the whole area would be an aquatic pesthole rife with disease, unless something was done to clear it out.

In the early afternoon, Bar-Woten accompanied the first boat to go ashore. They scrambled up a sagging wooden dock that had been driven half its length ashore and stood on the crumbling remains of the log and brick bund. A few birds scolded them from the naked tree as they walked on the ragged roadway inland.

The waves had burrowed up the inland passage with concentrated force, leaving the hills spattered with mud and twisted foliage. But the water had spent its force against the great stone boulder that formed a partial gateway to the valley of Mappu. It had coursed down the highway and spilled into the river that ran through the city. Mappu itself looked a little shaken and some of its buildings were cracked and leaning precariously, but on the whole it had survived well. Only a few islanders had stayed in the city, however, the old or very young, and they looked dazed, with wild, staring eyes. They could only point and say everyone had gone to Dat.

The shore party halted at the palace gates and reconnoitered. Bar-Woten and three others were instructed by the first mate to take the dirt path to the eastern peninsula about ten kilometers away and see how many islanders were actually at the statues. The others would go deeper into the valley and determine how many had hidden in the inland caves beyond Mappu.

Dark clouds stacked to the south and rushed with unusual haste toward the island. Bar-Woten watched thunderheads grow, visibly billowing and darkening. Sheets of silent lightning played between them.

The party marched through thick, buggy jungle when the first downpour hit. Taking shelter beneath a broad, leafy ironwood tree, they waited as marble-sized drops of water pummeled the forest and roadway. The storm abated to a fine drizzle, fading the trees into rustling gray giants and decorating the leaves with crystal beads. The bird noises resumed. Insects rose in puffs and blasts, haunting every step in the ankle-deep mud. Large spiders, red and tan, crossed the path with high-prancing steps and challenged the hikers with raised forelimbs. The Ibisian forged ahead and shooed them aside with a broken palm frond. In a few minutes the end of the frond was sticky with webbing.

Two of the party were women, one middle-aged and graying with knotted muscles on her arms and calves, tough as any man; the other slender and young with a close-cut shag of hair. The second man was an engine-watch officer, ten years younger than Bar-Woten, but just as knowledgeable in the ways of jungles. They swapped short, breathless stories on jungle life. Bar-Woten told of the years he'd spent in the Pais Vermagne, searching for the city of the Firstborn. It was the first any had heard of his long trek, and they asked lots of questions, some of them pointed. He deftly avoided incriminating answers.

The path emerged on a white sand beach that had avoided the major impact of the deluge. They walked across the hard-packed, damp sand for a half hour, then crossed a muddy jungle stream from the hills. The path picked up again a few steps beyond and led them over a rise into the valley where the statues stood.

Dat had been imposing from the sea; now she was overwhelming. The waves had toppled one of her guardians. The serpent column lay at her feet, half-buried in mud and foliage. Seated in silence around the valley, on the fallen column, at the base of Dat, and even on the crest of the cliffs twenty or thirty meters higher, were at least ten thousand people. They stared with wide, clear eyes at the goddess's face, hands folded in their laps. The tiny king and queen sat among them, incense bearers nearby.

Bar-Woten sat on an unoccupied rock and motioned for the others to follow his example. Together they stared at Dat and thought their own thoughts.

They were all lucky to be alive.

Kiril's chest was tightly wrapped with bandages, and it hurt to breathe. There was a funny dislocated feeling around his shoulders. He couldn't focus both eyes on a single object for very long. Vague shapes moved around him in the dark.

I'm in the infirmary, he told himself. Something happened to me. I might have fallen down stairs. Slipped.

He remembered nothing about the waves.

He dreamed fuzzy dreams for a long time — months it seemed — about riding the balloons in Mediweva, reading the Obelisk texts, meeting and becoming friendly with and loving Elena, spending afternoons in the park around the promenade in the village of Gidalha, where the birds sang even past dark and the air smelled of frangipani from the village censers breathing out their holiday smells.

He talked to the doctor and his nurse occasionally, but there were a lot of small injuries to be treated, and cases much more serious than his own. Bar-Woten and Barthel were both on the island, so he spent most of his time alone.

The sounds of riveting and hammering and sawing came to him day and night. He slowly remembered what had happened.

He overheard that one third of Golumbine's population, seventeen thousand people, had died in the waves. Most of the native boats had been swamped at sea or wrecked ashore. Twenty crewmen on the *Trident* had been badly hurt and three were dead.

He slept. He led a disjointed existence for two weeks.

108

The day finally came when he was allowed to walk by himself and go on deck. He looked north. It was still gray, but the south was bright and warm and inviting. The island was disheveled, with an intent, serious look of recovery. People repaired the docks and bund. Long lines carried pails of bricks and mortar back and forth in an endless stream. Masons applied and cemented, working by torchlight at night.

The smell of death was almost gone. Boats still cruised the harbor, dredging for bodies and taking them out to sea for deep-water burial. The majority of the flotsam had been salvaged for rebuilding boats. Only a few floating tree trunks provided a hazard to navigation. The water was a clear blue-green again.

The weather had changed. Winds from the north were colder, and everyone on the *Trident* knew that meant only one thing. The Obelisk that had once risen high over Weggismarche and Pallasta and the other countries below the Pale Seas was now gone. What that had done to the *Trident*'s homeland none could say — but they weren't optimistic.

The very thought that an Obelisk could fall was shaking. Added to the starry sky of nine months past, it meant nothing was going to be as it had been. But how many more disasters would hit them?

Kiril had known things were awry for two and a half years, ever since Elena had been changed. It was a matter of escalation, not beginnings.

The *Trident* needed repairs which would take at least two months. In that time those who weren't directly involved with the work were given leave to help on the island. Shoreline communities had to be rebuilt from the ground up, and in some cases repopulated.

In the wake of the disaster the island no longer mourned.

Rather a mood of frenetic work prevailed. By some fluke there were more men on the island than women now, by about two to one. This didn't conflict with the past at all, as polyandry had been an accepted practice. But it created a host of problems for the men.

Kiril spent his last days of recovery touring the island, walking or riding on the half-repaired roads, and visiting the sites where the *Trident*'s crew was helping rebuild.

He stayed for two days in Mappu as a consultant in reshelving the religious library. The second day he sat in the tumble of stone shelves and scrolls with a group of priest-initiates and explained the practice of setting up a card catalog, stumbling between Teutan and rudimentary Golumbine.

A black-haired, umber-skinned woman entered the library and snapped her fingers commandingly. They all looked up, Kiril frowning. She wore a sari-like dress that covered her from ankle to shoulder. Her expression was mild and gentle, and when she spoke she used the proper words of apology, but she obviously expected their complete attention.

A formal choosing of husbands would begin at dusk in Mappu's ritual plaza. All unchosen males were required to be there. She added, with a neutral glance at Kiril, that foreigners were also invited. "The obligations, in any case, will be temporary," she explained to him in Teutan. Then she smiled, turned delicately, and walked out.

It was the last thing Kiril wanted to be involved in. The initiates buzzed with interest and speculation. It took him some minutes to bring the discussion back to the catalog.

Bar-Woten and Barthel walked across the half-finished bund and hired a taxi to take them to the ritual plaza. They were passing through a side street in Mappu, their driver hissing his animal on and flapping the reins, when they saw Kiril.

They ordered the taxi to stop and invited him to join them. He was too tired to think much about where they were going. He assumed they were on their way to supper. He climbed into the carriage, and the taxi picked up speed.

The ritual plaza was a broad, open square paved in ochre stone bricks, with a deep communal cistern at its center and a rise of stone seats at one end. Thousands of years ago the plaza had been the scene of sacrifices, whether animal or human the Golumbines were reluctant to say. Now it served as a civic center when the island council met.

The seats were filled with bustling and chattering women, dressed in ceremonious red and green wrappings, their hair flowing over their shoulders and their eyes bright with interest. The plaza was empty, but crowds of men clustered at both sides looking anxious and nervous. The taxi let the three out at the edge of the plaza, Kiril realized they weren't going to dinner.

"What are we doing here?" he asked quietly. Bar-Woten grinned and said nothing. Too tired to put up any fuss, he stood with them, willing to watch the proceedings but not to participate. His ribs still ached a little.

The late afternoon was still warm and sultry. Birds squawked in the jungle beyond the plaza's boundary. A tall priest dressed in green walked to the top of the wall around the well and called for order in a loud, clear voice. When he had everybody's attention he told the crowd on all three sides that the choosing could begin.

Kiril wearily tried to find a hint of moral fault with what was going on, but couldn't. He'd seen too much grief and misery in the streets of Mappu in the last few weeks to grudge this organic respite. There was anxiety in the crowd, but also joy and anticipation. He couldn't visualize what the result would be — a series of ritual marriages? Or arranged orgies to stimulate a new, fresh tide of children? It all seemed very remote. He watched with objective interest.

The men at the opposite side of the plaza stepped forward and arranged themselves in front of the stone seats, each standing two steps from his neighbor to be seen clearly. The first row of women went among the men and looked over them sharply, haggling with each other. For a spectator it wasn't entrancing. All together about six thousand people filled the plaza, with twice as many men as there were women.

The haggling continued until dusk. Torches set in stands along the plaza lighted the proceedings. The women made their choices from the first group. About three hundred men went away unchosen.

Golumbine priests then urged the second group to take its position. Kiril was caught up in the crowd, something he hadn't bargained for, and was pushed forward despite his protests. "I'm not supposed to be here," he said, but the men surrounding him thought he was only trying to find a better frontline position. Bar-Woten was lost in the press, and he couldn't see them.

He shrugged his coat back onto his shoulders. It was useless. No one would choose him anyway. The men fell quiet as the women started to pass among them. Most of the women smiled at Kiril, but paid little attention — he was from the *Trident*, not a native. It wasn't wise to get involved with a sailor.

He felt depressed after an hour under the dark sky. Few fire doves were visible. Brighter ones would blink into view in a few minutes, and others would rise, but for the moment it was dark with only torchlight to guide the women.

One girl a few years younger than Kiril stopped and tried to talk to him. It was no good. He knew very little dialect,

112

and she knew nothing in Teutan beyond amenities. She looked him over frostily and moved on.

Irritated and nervous he shifted on his feet and wondered when it would be over. His legs were aching and his chest itched beneath his bandages.

Another women stepped up to examine him. He held out his arm when asked, then blinked and looked at her more closely. She was the woman who'd made the announcement in the library and spoke excellent Teutan. She asked how he was feeling.

"Fine," he said, his mouth dry. She inspected him like a doctor, but with less coarseness than the other women. Finally she took his hand and put it on her waist, the signal she had chosen him.

"But I'm not in the — the competition," he said.

"Come with me."

He passed Bar-Woten, who raised an eyebrow, then grinned broadly and grunted deep in his throat.

"Damn you!" Kiril whispered. "Get me out of this!"

"I am Ual," the woman said. "I like you because I think you're probably pretty smart. You smart?"

"Dumb as an ox," Kiril said.

"I don't *think* so!" she said, her voice rising to a pretty peak.

"I'll have to go back on the ship, so this is all useless."

She shook her head, no, and he suddenly found himself willing. Something simply snapped and he caught the spirit, and his body grew warm and he liked the touch of her hand.

"You'll be excused for a while," she said. "You work here now anyway."

They left the plaza and followed a twisting, dark road through Mappu. Hundreds of fire doves were out like glowing insects now. He wanted to take her then and there, with an insane pressure he could hardly control. But she kept his hand loosely in hers and led him through a gate into a courtyard.

"I don't feel too well," something made him say. She smiled back, and he knew he was lying.

Fourteen

The inside of the courtyard was paved with tile and had a fountain in the middle, a bronze dish supported by stone lions so old they were almost shapeless. Lamplight came through the upper windows of the house at the end of the yard. A jagged crack ran from the rounded top of the door frame to a window above. It all looked as old as the fountain. Next to it, Ual was as fresh and young as a flower.

They went through the door and stood in a hallway across the front of the house, doors at either end. He asked why the hall had no door in the middle, and she said that was to keep the *gingerii* out — demons. Demons could only travel in a straight line. She quickly demonstrated that there was no way a demon could get from the door to the end of the hall in a straight line in either direction. Kiril nodded. She led him to the right and opened the door with an iron key tied around her waist.

She left him standing alone in a small, bare room with a window at eye level in the outer wall. He sat on a smooth wooden bench, crossing his legs. Elena came to mind, and he frowned. Something feral was working in him. He turned his guilt into a kind of anger at Elena; she had no right to expect him to be inhumanly chaste.

"This is the household of my brother, Hualao," she told him when she returned. "He died in the waves." Kiril apologized, and she looked at him curiously.

"You had nothing to do with it."

115

"But I'm sorry he's dead."

"If he wasn't dead, you wouldn't be here. Your ship would have sailed away, and I'd have never even thought about choosing you."

Kiril nodded, though he didn't understand. He followed her into a high-ceilinged room filled with a stone hearth, a heavy plush rug, and comfortably padded rattan furniture.

"I'm a virgin," she said. He nodded agreeably until he realized what she'd said. He felt stupid and clumsy. This was a sensuous ocean island — weren't all girls soon experienced here? His nervousness trebled.

"But you won't be able — " he began to say.

"Hm?"

"I'm sorry," he said.

"You're sorry all the time."

"I'll be sleeping out here," he said. In Mediweva husbands always spent the first few nights sleeping separately from their wives. It supposedly built up friendship and confidence and confirmed the relationship in the eyes of God.

"You'll be cold. You don't want to sleep out here."

"Why did you choose me? I can't stay in Golumbine. I'd make a very poor husband."

"You don't like me?" she asked. "I'm very likable. Lots of men want me."

"I like you — I want you very much."

"You don't sound sure."

"How old are you, Ual?"

"Marriage age."

"I mean, how many years?"

"That is one word I've never been able to understand."

They took seats next to each other on a divan with cotton cushions. Kiril told her what a year was, and she laughed. Without Obelisk texts to influence a person, Hegira was virtually timeless, divided only into night and day. Seasons weren't important when the prevailing winds were warm and the currents brought a tropical surge day in, day out.

"I am many, many days old," she said. "I must be many years old, maybe fifty."

"No," he said. "You can't be fifty. I'd say you're about twenty. Maybe twenty-two."

"That must be your age."

"About," he said. "I'm twenty-one, very young."

"Marriage age."

"But I can't stay."

"That's okay. I will have many other husbands, perhaps before you leave."

He held his hands together between his knees and swallowed. He'd almost forgotten. Something ached inside him, and it wasn't his healing rib cage.

"I'm not used to that, Ual," he said. "Where I come from, a man can only have one wife."

"Same here, sometimes," she said.

"But a woman can only have one husband."

"Oh." She looked at his hands and put her hand on them. "Listen. I am an important woman here. Lots of men want to marry me. But I am important enough I won't need to have more husbands until after you go. Ship will stay here another . . . " she paused. "Thirty or forty days. Part of a year. I can wait. I like you enough to wait."

He didn't know what to do. But someone inside of him did. He held her hand up to his and kissed it. It reminded him of kissing Elena's hand, but not in an unpleasant way. It was as if all women were wonderfully the same, with the same ability to soothe and attract . . . and to hurt terribly if he didn't handle things right. If he did something wrong. He felt very mixed up, but wonderful. "I'm honored," he whispered.

"That's the way," she said. "Now I know why I picked you. You're a virgin too!"

Kiril opened and closed his mouth like a fish. He resented her implication all the more because it was true. He looked at her steadfastly. "Why would you want to choose a virgin? Both of us will be stumbling in the dark."

"There will be no advantages . . . Both will learn."

She had moved no closer to him, but the heat of her body and her subtle perfume were already bothering him. There were many texts on the Obelisks that gave intimate details of the love habits of the First-born. There was no reason to think things were any different on the far island of Golumbine. But did they kiss with their lips?

It was necessary for him to find out.

They did, and apparently by long tradition.

He was still nervous as she stroked the back of his neck and nibbled at his nose. But he noted with some pride that it wasn't a debilitating anxiety. He knew little about disrobing a young woman, but Golumbine's fashions weren't nearly as difficult to remove as Mediweva's had been. He ruefully remembered having tried several times with Elena. If the stays and girdles had been less restraining she might have given in. But he had been ham-handed and both had retreated in discouragement.

Ual did not retreat. She helped. He grew accustomed to her willingness, but it took some time to get used to her unnerving familiarity with his own clothing and his own person.

He thought of Elena, not with guilt, but with a sharp, grieving pain. By rights this should have been her night, her privilege — their privilege — and not the smiling, willing joy of an umber-skinned woman in a land Elena had never heard of. Knowing this, and feeling the stab, he understood with more than his mind that he had no choice.

All of Golumbine was demanding a rebirth. Who was he to resist? He went with her to a room illuminated by small oil lamps, where there was a thick, soft mattress woven of rattan and cotton yarn covered with a sheet of fine linen. The sheet was printed with blocks and circles of purple and brown. As she removed her final garment, a small pair of pants with a skirt around them, and turned to face him, he felt his entire chest alternately weakening and growing strong with the push-pull of his heart and lungs. It was a flutter he'd never felt before, a thick-running excitement that was a mixture of terror and pride.

He was afraid of hurting her. She pulled him down, her eyes so dark in the dim lamplight that he couldn't see their whites, just narrow gaps of brown, almost black.

Later, her hips and thighs crimsoned, she took his hand and moved him off the bed. She gathered up the cloth and cut it into small strips with a sharp knife. Then in the sitting room she soaked it in oil and put it in the fire. She squatted before it, an awesome, youthful idol, flames mirrored in her eyes.

She cleaned both of them off with a soft wet rag and spread another sheet like the first. Kiril found it hard to go to sleep quickly. He stayed awake an hour or more longer than Ual, staring into the dark.

Fifteen

Birds rose from the lake, pink and white and midnight blue,
as Bar-Woten plunged his paddle into the water and scooted
the reed boat along. Jungle circled the lake and even extended
onto it on long legs of twisted roots. Birds and aquatic lizards
flocked across the roots in squawking conflict. The sky was a
hot, pale blue. The north was no longer dark. Through a
smoked glass a bright band of light could be seen extending
from the western Obelisk and widening to form an ovoid
where the northern Obelisk had been.

A head with glittering, opalescent eyes rose in the water
where he was about to dip his paddle, making him jerk his
arm back. The head vanished, and water sprayed with the
swish of a tail. This was no lake for unaided swimmers.
Insects as long as a finger scurried over it and dipped below
to pierce small fish and tadpoles with wicked mandibles.
They could just as easily bite through an unwary hand.
White snakes — a delicate side dish for the Golumbines —
gathered in floating lacework colonies to swim and bask.

The lake was a soup of life. It was tepid and brackish at
one end, clogged with leech-infested reeds and matted algae.
It did not smell too offensive because the wind was fresh and
strong. The wind dried off the sweat of his paddling and
made the jungle hum and whistle. Drifts of spider web
floated from the trees.

He brought the boat up onto a dirt embankment and
pulled it out of the water. Then he sat on a mossy rock to

think. His foot found a hold in the spotted gray stone, and he bent to examine the niche. It was more than a rock — it was a head. Worn gray eyes peered at him, eyebrows cracked and covered with lichen. The stone nose was half-buried in thick damp soil. Ageless idols were not rare here, but the head still fascinated him. He had often dreamed of exploring long-deserted cities. Perhaps temples existed in the jungle that could begin to slake that thirst. But the deep jungle wasn't recommended for inexpert visitors.

He had borrowed the boat and crossed the lake to find a place to sit and think alone and in relative silence. But now that he was alone, he couldn't concentrate. His mind kept drifting off into the past, but that way led to blood and cruelty and mind-blanked hatred. It also reminded him of a great love for Sulay.

He still felt sad for Sulay. The memories welled up, and he couldn't put them aside: The day he had fought with the bear and lost his eye, and that evening as the surgeons had bandaged him . . . Sulay had stood over him in the dark and firelight with the dark forest all around, chuckling and reassuring. "You're Bear-killer now . . . Woten would be proud, and so would the Thunder-Bearer, Eloshim."

Years later, as an aide to the general, he had been given the pick of the captured Khemites to choose a servant from. Tired from the fighting and feeling dirty with blood and self-anger, Bar-Woten had recognized a face among the children. Barthel — "Servant of Bar," originally named Amma bin Akka — had been small, dark, and scrappy with more spirit and fear and hate than Bar-Woten had ever thought he could control. But the young Khemite had taken to Bar-Woten as if to a second father, imitating him and absorbing all he had to teach, although retaining his Momadan faith. For years Bar-Woten had trusted the Khemite not to plunge a knife

121

into his back. There was good reason for him to try, Bar-Woten knew — but the Khemite didn't know.

And Bar-Woten would never tell, because his stomach heaved at the memory. It was just as well that Barthel had hidden under reed baskets that day in Khem and seen so little.

An insect crawled up his leg, and he let it climb onto his finger, chancing that it might sting or prick, but it did nothing, and he set it off on the jungle floor.

He brought out his leather pouch and ate. What was most terrible of all was that he didn't feel nearly as guilty as he should. He took his pain with a sort of zest. He knew he could repeat the past at any time, because though forbidding, it wasn't nearly as frightening as what lay ahead. Establishing familiar territory in the future was necessary, even though the landmarks should be blood and destructions.

Bar-Woten shook his head slowly, chewing on his piece of fruit. He packed his waste into the leather pouch and put the boat in the river to continue his journey.

Golumbine offered any number of marvels to the casual eye. There were deep green gorges slashed by long plumes of waterfalls where circular rainbows dazzled. There were multicolored reptile herds, some carnivorous but most not, that stalked through the forest on their hind feet, hunting or browsing on the lower branches and ferns. Butterflies as wide as two hands thumb-to-thumb bobbed in and out of shadow. There were marble quarries and quartz hillsides.

And there was Mappu itself, where men were in abundance, and neither he nor Barthel found themselves in much demand. He smiled at that, thinking of Kiril's distress.

He was envious. He'd grown a little bored with the women of the *Trident*.

*

122

Barthel looked at the maps laid out before him on a forecastle capstan and drew his finger along the Bicht of Weggismarche. There was a small circle that showed the former position of the Obelisk. He used a pencil to sketch in the probable path of the fall.

Their trade route took them through several broad curves from Golumbine to southern Weggismarche. Depending on what they found after delivering their chief cargo — saffron and several other ton-lots of spice — they'd make a brief journey into the Pale Seas to pick up goods in the port of Dambapur, the farthest northern city of Weggismarche's tiny sister-state, Nin. Then they'd sail with the currents to the southeast and begin another long circle, which, in five or six years, would again end in Weggismarche.

If there was nothing left of Weggismarche their plans would have to change, of course. At any rate Barthel knew that Bar-Woten, Kiril, and himself would probably leave the ship before then. They might travel along the coast of the Pale Seas, though the map showed little of what lay in those regions beyond a cursory trace of probable coastal zones.

He was reluctant to leave the *Trident*. He'd learned a lot on the ship and gained some independence from the Bey by being able to do his own work and think his own thoughts. But his loyalty was still too strong to break. He'd go where the Bey went, and Kiril probably would as well.

He had seen Kiril with his "wife" the day before at one of Mappu's vegetable markets. Kiril had appeared contented. That puzzled Barthel. Changes in men's moods or mores always puzzled him. The Bey had been the way he was since Barthel had known him, given allowances for times and strenuous circumstances. But Kiril, closer to Barthel's age, seemed much more changeable. Barthel wondered if he himself could show fluctuations as broad. He didn't think so.

Work on the port hull of the *Trident* was nearly finished. In a few weeks the ship would be ready to leave, and they'd all have to detach themselves from Golumbine. He was glad he didn't have many detachments to make.

Captain Prekari made his usual midafternoon inspection of the repairs, carrying rolls of ship's plans in metal tubes, as Bar-Woten came aboard. He went to his cabin and saluted the captain in passing, dropped his goods on the narrow double bunk he shared with Barthel — who took the upper berth — and went aft to shower under freshwater pumps. He didn't trust the baywater yet. No one did. The saltwater pumps were detached for the time they'd spend in the harbor.

He soaked himself down and used lye soap to scrub off.

Kiril came aboard two hours later, haggard and irritable. Barthel showed him the map course but didn't ask any questions. The evening meal was quiet. Those who had worked all day on the ship and those who had been ashore all day looked equally fatigued.

Just after dusk Kiril lay on a lower berth in the cabin he shared with three other men and listened to someone striking up a dance with pipes and tambourine on the quarterdeck. He was too tired to think, though Ual came to mind before he went to sleep. He had been helping two of her half-brothers repair the cracks in the house that day. It had taken a great deal of mortar mixing and masonry, and his hands were raw. He had told her he had to be on board this evening for watch, too weary to face the planned family festivities after the day was done. Still, just before sleep, he missed her warmth and wished he had stayed behind.

He dreamed about walking with Elena to the temple of Dat in the older section of Mappu. She offered up torn strips of cloth, and the statue bent to accept them with a flaming hand. The statue was not dark-bronze, but mirror-bright silver; and the cloth strips turned to ice and melted away in the flames, hissing. He woke in the morning with a drained feeling and wondered what Elena would have been doing, in any case, on Golumbine.

The morale of the ship was at a low ebb. They had no idea what had happened in Weggismarche, whether there was any country to return to or not. They feared not.

Some fights broke out, and the animosities they caused were difficult to settle. The captain avoided direct contact with the crew, which Bar-Woten knew was a standard tactic in times of unresolvable tension. Work on the ship slowed somewhat, and the quality of the work declined.

More and more of the crew were withdrawn from helping the Golumbines and assigned to repair details on the *Trident*, allowing shorter shifts. Kiril sweated for a day the possibility he would be withdrawn also, but he remained.

At midday, his library instruction duties over, he went to Ual's clan home and helped fix the family meal. It was everybody's duty to contribute something to the late afternoon repast. Kiril was no good as a cook, so he helped with the cleaning and basic preparation of the raw food. Ual and one sister did most of the cooking.

The family was huge by any standard. The relations of the various members to each other were difficult to understand and impossible for Kiril to remember. He stumbled along as best he could and tried to keep his astonishment and indignation in check. Family standards for breeding were much looser than in Mediweva. Dat, he learned from Ual, was the product of her own extratemporal union with the ocean god, Nepheru-Shaka. She was her own mother then, and her own daughter. Nepheru-Shaka was conceived (again out of time) by Dat and the island god, Ashlok — both of whom were female, but Ashlok less definitely so. From this Trinity —

with Ashlok as the only unbegotten and unexplained part —
came all the other forces, *gingerii*, minor gods, and the
seventy-nine Notions that comprised the loose pantheon of
Golumbine. It was a very intellectual religion, quite static.
By any definition of culture the Golumbine population should
have crumbled into formless bands and gone through the
agonies of cultural renaissance long ago. But the culture was
stable and showed no signs of decay. Kiril, struggling to
ignore the lessons of First-born history as recorded on the
Obelisks, speculated the Golumbines were flexible in other
ways. Certainly the family group was flexible. They seemed
to follow the example of their gods — first cousins were
allowed to marry; even, in certain circumstances, brother
and sister.

The generic name of Ual's family was Punapilhi, with the
ending "hi" whistled. Within that group name, seldom used,
were other names denoting people living together under one
roof, people wishing to be named as a subgroup for various
reasons, associations of artisans within the family, and other
relations that escaped Kiril.

Ual herself was directly involved with family planning.
She was a representative in what the *Trident*'s crew called
"the Rebirth Committee." Its main function was to keep
Golumbine's diverse family groups together and encourage
the production of healthy children. They had a crude but
surprisingly effective method of family counseling on good
breeding. To an extent this made them matchmakers.

Ual's natural father accepted Kiril without comment. Ual
had several family fathers — her natural father was not even
her favorite. All her fathers — and at one count Kiril found
six — had been husbands to her mother, who was a pleasant,
plump old woman, no great beauty now, but handsome and
jovial. Kiril took a shine to her.

Ual treated Kiril in public like a favorite brother, and in

private little differently, but with extended liberties. His state of husbandship was not stressed, nor formalized by ritual, for he wasn't yet a father. She didn't discourage him from setting up relationships with other females in the family group, but Kiril had no inclination to do so. The whole arrangement was at times a strain on him. After a month of "marriage," he slept aboard the *Trident* more often. He disliked himself for not fitting in, but he knew the reasons why. His whole being was alien to their way of life.

It was difficult to face the fact — a very un-Kristian fact — that there were many ways of being happy, prosperous, and pious in human experience. Some of those ways contradicted one another.

As his disenchantment increased, his love for Ual also increased. Halfhearted, sick with conflict, he struggled with himself. He couldn't let things ride until the *Trident* offered her own solution. He had to act sooner.

Ual did not become pregnant in the first month. Her period came, something Kiril knew very little about, and she was sequestered until the menstrual flow had ceased. This had never been the custom in Mediweva, but Kiril accepted it. It gave him time to think clearly.

When she came out of seclusion, her work with the Rebirth Committee absorbed her for a few more days. They saw very little of each other. Then Kiril managed to pull her away from her omnipresent family, from her position on the Committee, but not from her preoccupation with thoughts of both. At first she only half listened as he tried to explain his difficulties.

They sat in the empty vegetable market of Mappu in the late afternoon of a religious holiday. A faint breeze scattered bits of dried twigs and leaves across the ground, sounding like the tick of dogs' claws on pavement. He told her he was finding it hard to be happy.

127

"You've said nothing before," she told him.

"I've been trying to explain it to myself. I can't."

"Because you're going, that's why you're unhappy."

"That may be. But also because I can't fit into what you do, with your family and all. I'm a wanderer, but I have a lot of solid things in my life that keep me from being like you."

"Oh," she said. "But you leave soon anyway. Enjoy while you can."

He shook his head. It was impossible to explain.

"I would like one thing," Ual said quietly, looking up at him to watch his reaction. "I would like to take advantage of an offer that will be helpful when you leave. A man has offered to be a husband to me, and the alliance of our families would be desirable."

"After I'm gone you won't have to ask for permission."

"I would marry him before, but I made a promise to you. You would have to release me from that."

Kiril stared at her.

"He will not be a mating husband until after you've gone," she assured him.

He was scandalized. "I can't allow that," he said, knowing he was being despicable. "That's not right."

"But we love each other now."

"You love ME!"

"Yes."

"Then why don't you try to stop me from going?"

"I like you. I won't stop you on your path."

"But if you loved me you'd try to keep me for as long as you could."

"I love the pictures in the sky at night when the fire doves draw," she said. "But I can't stop them from changing, and each night they are different."

"There has to be something, something *wrong* when two

people don't wish to have each other for as long as they can."

"I do want you."

"Not forever."

"I'm not sure of that word. I've studied it. I don't think there is a forever."

"As long as we live."

"Ah! But after we die, Dat makes sure we never meet again in other bodies to mate. It is a rule of nature that all things must leave each other. I cannot fight that. You cannot. Nepheru-Shaka will take you away to Weggismarche, and you will have things to do there."

Kiril had nothing to say. His brain was a knot of thoughts, all of them valid, all ridiculous.

"And you have told me," Ual continued, "that you have to rescue a person you love very deeply. I cannot stop you from that."

"Ual, that has nothing to do with — " He stopped himself.

It did. It had everything to do with what he was doing now. He didn't care about Elena now. He wanted only Ual, and he wanted her away from her family, away from Bar-Woten and Barthel, from the *Trident*, even from Golumbine, away in some nowhere without conflict. That was the only way he could have her, keep her, the way he wanted her. Kiril knew that was hopelessly immature and destructive. It hurt that he couldn't stop himself from wanting it.

They would destroy each other even in ideal circumstances. She was like a fish out of water when isolated from her family. Taken away from the journey to find Elena's double, he would be a stripling youth again, without strength or purpose. He would wander from life to life and probably not find happiness even in the best of times with Ual.

He held his hands out in front of him in a shrug and told

129

her it couldn't go on. "I don't feel right about it," he said. She became exasperated.

"You don't know what love is!" she said. "You want everything to last forever."

He nodded.

"So you would stop us from loving now, from helping to rebuild, because you will leave. I don't understand that."

There was nothing for him to do but get angry. "You'll have a dozen husbands after me," he said, his voice grinding low in his throat. "Why don't you just forget me, write me off as a bad job?"

"You are senseless now," she said.

"No doubt. It hurts me to do this."

"It hurts me to watch you."

They sat in the shade of a wide, tall fern in the vegetable market and looked at each other for a few seconds. Kiril felt removed from time. The myriad pressures all added up to one push, which he was following as surely as an arrow flies from its string.

She stood up and started to walk away.

"No," Kiril said, reaching out to hold her hand. "I don't want you to go without understanding. I want to help both of us understand. You're the first woman I've ever had. I'm glad for that. You did nothing to hurt me. But after a while I'd be like a rock around your neck. You'd want to take other husbands, and I wouldn't let you. Even anticipating that makes me mad at myself, and with you. Because you can't be what I want you to be."

"Can anyone?" she asked, a quick coldness in her voice.

He spoke softly and his words were sure. "Not now. But you especially can't be. I think we have to leave each other. Let's not do it with bitterness."

"There is no other way," she said. "Otherwise we will not leave for good. A good hunter always makes a clean kill."

"Neither of us are hunting."

"You! You are hunting."

It had to end in anger or it would start up again; it had to be killed. He knew that was what Ual meant. She was turning her disappointment into indignation. Blaming him was the only way.

His shoulders dropped slightly. "I'm sorry," he said.

"You are always sorry."

Then she was gone, and the weight was gone, and something like clarity returned to his thoughts. But his shoulders wouldn't rise again, and he couldn't stand straight.

He returned to the *Trident*. The broken mast was being replaced and new rigging was being strung. Darkness came quickly, and candles and torches were lighted on the bund like processions of fire doves.

Sixteen

The *Trident* steamed out of the harbor with bright sky and calm water to greet her. Rust stained her hull in long red streaks and some of her sails were patchwork, but her engines were running smoothly and her methane tanks were full. To Bar-Woten she didn't sound the same — her squeaks and groans and snaps came from different areas with different rhythm — but she took the wind well when it came up. She was seaworthy again.

Golumbine drifted to the south. By evening they couldn't see the island any more. They were sailing into the dark blue seas that marked the northern waters of the Bicht av Genevar. Away from the warm currents surrounding Golumbine, the air grew chill. High clouds of ice crystals glowed overhead as the last of daylight faded; herringbone, mare's tail, lacework, and fly's wing. To Kiril it seemed sometimes as if cryptic messages were being written in the sky.

Barthel and Avra and two navigation officers studied the morning glare of the light above the fallen Obelisk, trying to determine how it grew bright and why it faded. Barthel had the uncomfortable feeling it was no natural thing they were watching — not the work of Allah, but something a shade less exalted, though no less impressive.

Bar-Woten worked for several days finding small leaks in the methane tanks. He worked silently, putting his whole body into it, glad to be traveling again. When his duty was over he went to the prow and stood with one foot resting on the bowsprit clamps, staring north with eye squinted, riddling what lay ahead. Sometimes he shivered and went to his cabin before darkness set in. None of what he saw in the hazy distance pleased him.

And nothing of what they found in the Bicht was encouraging. Most of the small islands were now barren deserts of sand and mud with patches of salt grass. The larger ones had been ravaged not only by waves and quakes, but by what looked like war. Entire villages had been haphazardly rebuilt, only to be put to the torch. No trade was possible when the only inhabitants were half-dead old women and belly-bloated children. The *Trident* gave aid where she could, but more often than not she had to leave at full speed with desperate rag-tag ships in pursuit.

The farther north they sailed, the more discouraged they became. The voyage had gone sour. The captain stayed isolated; all orders were relayed through the mates and deck officers. But the crew was too tired and beleaguered to complain or start trouble.

Barthel told himself, each time he saw misery and destruction, that the Obelisk's fall was Allah's method of testing the will of man. The will of man was not giving an encouraging performance.

In their twenty-ninth day out of Golumbine the first ship-on-legs appeared, gray, fast and sleek, lacking sails. No action was taken. The *Trident* maintained her course and pushed northward, sailing more each day into the ghoulish green light of the glowing patch in the sky. The pale luminosity, dim as light through clouds on a warm summer day, cast no shadows and did not glare from the sea or the ship's metal. Barthel was distinctly uneasy on deck facing that dismal, makeshift glow. Bar-Woten ignored it as much as possible.

But he didn't ignore the ship-on-legs. In the *Trident*'s

library he studied manuals on battle tactics at sea. He knew that Prekari was well-versed in handling ships under dangerous conditions. But Bar-Woten had never been in a position to learn how wars were conducted at sea, and he found the difference fascinating.

The *Trident* wasn't equipped for a heavy sea battle. She carried only three guns, one fore, one aft, and one mounted midships, just aft of the first funnel. She also carried loads of split and dried logs to put into the burners for heat during a battle. In emergencies her methane tanks were always sealed and padded, and she either ran under sail or steamed on wood.

They were approaching the southern coast of Pallasta when the submarine appeared. Kiril had read about them, but it was a shock to see one surface and follow two hundred meters astern, like a steel-clad whale. Prekari ordered gun crews ready and converted as quickly as possible from methane to wood. Smoke began to pour from the stacks. The stacks creaked and groaned, and deck officers supervised the loosening of the stack guy wires. The sails were furled, and the *Trident* picked up speed, testing her pursuer.

The submarine fell behind immediately and submerged. Prekari appeared on the quarterdeck walking from side to side and peering over the railing. Bar-Woten stayed below with the engines, nursing a rod that ran hot under the stress. His overalls were soon soaked with hot grease. The smell of burnt packing clogged his nose and he sneezed every few seconds, but he refused to go topside. He refused to acknowledge he was being hunted by something he couldn't see.

For seven hours they ran on alert. The sounding bobs showed no change. Prekari stayed on the quarterdeck in a folding chair and ate his dinner in silence. After finishing his last plate he wiped his mouth and beard with a linen napkin and ordered the crew to secure general quarters. They would continue to burn wood until the next morning, but otherwise the ship would run as usual until something new developed.

Bar-Woten went on deck as he finished his watch and looked at the fire doves hovering over the pitchy sea. The waters were less fertile now. Fish were seldom seen and seabirds were rare.

By the light of morning, gray and eerie, they saw the coast of Pallasta. It was a savage, burnt ribbon of black and brown. Weggismarche had had little peaceful commerce with Pallasta, a country dedicated to military discipline and rigid political regimes. Up until four decades ago, war had been almost continuous between them. It didn't look as if there would be any more wars. Kiril looked up and down the ragged coast and wondered why God would allow such destruction, and for what purpose. His heart grew bitter and his nose filled with the acrid smell of singed land and dead waters.

By now it should have been winter in Weggismarche and Pallasta. But the air was warm and humid, and the few mountains they could see were rocky and snowless.

The ship-on-legs reappeared two weeks after its first reconnaissance. The *Trident*'s crew watched it angrily, shouting and curling their hands into fists. Bar-Woten followed it with binoculars and noted it had guns on its deck. It rode with its hull out of water when it moved its fastest, but at other times it rode in the water like an ordinary ship, though still uncommonly fast.

Prekari kept the guns manned and put the ship on full alert again. He knew instinctively they would have to wait to be fired upon, if anyone was going to fire. The ship-on-legs had far more powerful weapons than the *Trident*. To provoke it would be insanity.

When the submarine surfaced in front of them, the crew shouted in rage and nearly went out of control. Prekari let them vent their feelings for a few minutes until they were hoarse, then ordered them back to their posts. The wood burners were stoked. The methane tanks were wrapped and secured with rubber-covered chains.

The submarine rose even higher in the water. A hatch opened in its sail. A bearded man stood behind the hatch, using it for protection, and rested a bull horn on top. He addressed them in a language they didn't understand. When he got no response he tried again, and still they understood nothing. He shook his head and disappeared. Kiril, stiff with tension, stood on the bow and tried to sound out the phrases and riddle them. They were familiar, but he couldn't place them. He hadn't studied all the Obelisk languages, but he'd gone over enough of them to recognize many of the words.

Two men appeared behind the open hatch. One slipped and almost went off the ribbed decking on the back of the sub. He regained his footing and looked through binoculars at the *Trident*, paying special attention to the flags that fluttered from her rigging fore and aft. Then he said something to his companion, and again the bull horn was brought up. The man spoke Teutan this time, muffled and with a heavy accent but recognizable.

"You are requested to follow us," he said. "You will be guided into port three days from here."

"That'll put us in the Pale Seas," Barthel told Kiril. Avra was beside him, her mouth set in a thin, grim line. Weggismarche sailors had always avoided the Pale Seas. Hegira, they said, did not behave there as it did everywhere else. At the terminus of the Pale Seas lay the Wall which determined the end of this section of the world. No one in recent memory had ever been there and returned.

Prekari's answer came by messenger from the quarterdeck. The first mate read the reply through a hailing cone.

"We thankfully decline and request leave to follow our own course."

The ship-on-legs drew nearer. Signal flags flew from its mast. Kiril couldn't read them, but Barthel could. "'Follow ship, or I will fire,' it says."

"There is no choice," the bull horn barked. "Follow or we will sink you."

Prekari kept his peace for fifteen minutes. Then he spoke, and the first mate hailed the sub again. "We will not allow a boarding party. We will follow you until fire dove Skhar reached thirty-three degrees ascension. After that we will discuss the issue."

Barthel smiled. There was no fire dove called Skhar, and no bright ones that would reach precisely thirty-three degrees in these waters. The captain was delaying.

"We do not understand the reference," the submarine said. "You will follow us, and there will be no further discussion."

Prekari gave the signal for all the guns to be loaded.

The ship-on-legs cut back its engines and fell slowly into the water, sliding behind the *Trident*. With the submarine in front and the ship-on-legs behind, there was little they could do. Prekari secured battle stations and ordered his mates to follow the submarine until further notice.

If they were heading into the Pale Seas, their course would take them past Pallasta's northern borders and Weggismarche. If there was nothing left in Weggismarche or Nin, then there was no reason why they shouldn't sail to the Wall itself. The first engine mate, a burly, hairy man, spoke to Bar-Woten as they watched from the poop deck.

"It's useless if we haven't got a home to come back to sometime or other," he said. He rolled his sleeves up and tied them with lengths of rope. "Let's go below and tend that rod. We're going to have to steam it up fine to follow

137

that thing, and the captain's bound to keep us on wood. No chance to rest and switch over."

In and out, steam and water and heat coursed. It was the only life and hope Bar-Woten recognized. He imagined them captured by unknown men; killed, perhaps. He fell into a black funk and watched the rod smoulder, making mechanical movements to cool and relieve it.

Seventeen

The coast of Weggismarche was covered with falling snow. Ships passed them going in several directions up and down the coast, but none were from Pallasta or Weggismarche. All came from the Pale Seas: fast, unknown, depressing. The air temperature fell so rapidly that frost and sea ice formed on the deck and rigging. At the same time humidity increased until they drifted through a freezing fog. All crew, on or off scheduled watches, worked to clear the deck and rigging of ice. Winter was coming late, but with a vengeance.

The fog obscured their view of most of Weggismarche. Perversely, hope rose among the crew that somehow their country had been spared the worst destruction of the Fall; that they might slip away when the fog was thick enough and return to their home. It would be a long battle with these men from the Pale Seas, they said, but it would be better than not knowing — it would be better than dying in sight of the Wall where the world ended.

Prekari stayed isolated.

Kiril made sketches of the submarine and ship-on-legs whenever it was clear enough to see them. After a few hours of peering through thinning fog and straining his eyes in the murky light, he had enough details to piece together what he thought the ship-on-legs looked like from all sides.

It had at least four small guns on each side and two large ones fore and aft. Tubes were mounted port and starboard, and banks of rectangular boxes squatted on the fantail.

Dishes studded a mast rising over the bridge. The vessel made a hideous roar when it was up to full speed and shot thin gray smoke from vents in the middle of the flat stern.

The submarine, what he could see of it, appeared to be fish-shaped, like a tuna, with a thickened fin directly behind its head. This tower, or sail, was gun-metal gray. The back of the sub was decked with dark varnished wood.

The second day of their capture took them past the northernmost peninsula of Weggismarche where the Obelisk had once stood. It lay on its side, spanning the isthmus like a bridge, buried in one mountain range on the peninsula and another on the continent, half its width lost in solid rock. It didn't appear broken as far as they could see, but the horizon swallowed its length in gray cloud. They passed the severed base of the Obelisk and saw it was smooth, as though cut by some unthinkable saw. The base thrust out beyond the mountain range of the peninsula and soared, a kilometer in the air, a square piece of chalk mounted on a rock-giant's ear. Where it had struck ground, flows of molten rock had cooled in curled gray rivers, some reaching to the sea. All around was charred desolation. Kiril looked at the destruction without any particular emotion. It was too incredible to believe. It seemed more likely that the Obelisk should have buried itself completely and been covered over.

The fallen spire was a monumental *thing*, like a stick thrust into an ant nest, its only purpose to stir up human lives. He loathed it and what it stood for — knowledge, gain, static civilizations, endless cyclopean achievement — all of it.

Hegira, too, had fallen in his eyes. The world was no longer self-evident axiom. It had to prove itself all over again before it could regain its solidity.

The submarine guided them into progressively shallower waters that changed color from deep blue-gray to gray-green.

The waves took on a dismal milky sheen. The air became dry and very cold. And nowhere, besides the ships that escorted them, did they see any signs of life.

They were in the Pale Seas.

On the fourth day, land appeared off the port bow. It was a narrow spit of sandy beach shrouded with thick ground fog. "It's embarrassed to show itself," Bar-Woten commented. Dusty green bushes dotted its northern slopes. It passed to stern by midday. By evening, on the starboard, sheer cliffs of reddish stone rose from the muddy sea. Birds wheeled around the waterline in white puffs. Their cries sounded like children mourning. A hooked and baited line dropped over the side brought up a small, almost featureless smeltlike fish, silvery when first pulled from the water, but milk white in death.

The submarine guided them into a barren, rocky harbor on the eighth day of their capture. They were ordered to drop anchor and await further instructions from the ship-on-legs, which was called a "hydrofoil." The submarine submerged and moved deeper into the harbor.

The captain ordered a sample taken from the water, and a cup was lowered over the side bringing up a liter of silty liquid. Prekari tentatively dipped his finger into it and tasted a drop. "It's not salty now," he said. "We're not in an ocean at all. We must be in a river."

Parts of the puzzle of the Pale Seas began to fall into place. From a few hundred kilometers north of Weggismarche on, the Pale Seas were actually one enormous river delta, conveying mud and silt from lands thousands of kilometers beyond. But the size of the river was staggering — where was its source? At the Wall?

Barthel learned from Avra why few Weggismarche sailors had ever traveled into the Pale Seas, and none as far as this. More than legends of unknown danger the Pale Seas were periodically flooded with a poisonous discharge, noxious gases rising from the effluent and discouraging passage. The peninsular Obelisk, it was assumed, marked a boundary line, since no other Obelisks could be seen to the north. What that implied, no one knew. But to the inhabitants of Weggis-marche, Pallasta, and the lands around them, the north was obviously inhospitable. Yet now they had proof that people lived there.

The ship-on-legs hailed them by late afternoon and instructed them to weigh anchor. They were going to leave the harbor and sail against the current. Fortunately, the wind would be with them.

By evening they saw smoke and haze. They pushed at full steam against the relentless water, sails taking a stiff breeze and masts and spars creaking with the strain. An unpleasant odor rose to greet them, subtler but more acrid than the single smell of the methane tanks. It stung the nostrils and made the eyes water.

From the distant shore, plumes of smoke rose from a colonnade of stacks. The air was filled with grease and soot. A brief, unpleasant thought occurred to Kiril — they were heading into hell, and fire and ice lay beyond.

The night was sleepless and unpleasant. As they lay at anchor in a small inlet, outside the swirling current, the darkness filled with the roar of machines and the bellow of furnaces. The wind had dropped and now smoke drifted thick about them, a foggy pall slowly closing in to suffocate. Barthel confessed he didn't like it at all. The trio met on the main deck at midnight and talked about what they'd do if they had to abandon ship. Barthel was reluctant to think about that; Kiril, on the other hand, was almost anxious. "I don't see any other chance," he said. "We'd be better off on our own now — "

"How's that?" Bar-Woten asked. "We don't know the

local language, or what type of people live here, or anything we'd need to know if we wanted to slip by unnoticed. I'm frightened by these machines — I'll admit that and laugh at anyone who says he isn't."

"You've lost the spirit of the thing. We're supposed to proceed whenever possible," Kiril said.

The Ibisian examined Kiril in the dim glow of their covered lantern. The Mediwevan stared into the dark.

"Not when we walk into an open fire instead of around it," Barthel said, shifting from his seat of ropes to the wooden deck. Kiril snorted.

"Listen," Bar-Woten hissed. "If this ship gets into a position no one can escape from, then we are trapped, too, and that's no good, I'll admit. We'll have to avoid that. But for the moment we can only wait and see. If the people who run the machines are as wise as they are clever, we may be better off than we think."

A whistle blasted beyond the hills surrounding the inlet. It sounded like a dying saurian. Kiril sweated profusely, though the night air was almost freezing.

"So we do nothing," he said. "We sit and wait to die and give it all up."

Bar-Woten turned to the glowing night air beyond the hills and licked his dry lips.

Eighteen

The morning was obscured by fog. It would be a bad time to cut and run in unfamiliar territory. Most of the *Trident*'s crew waited on deck for the fog to clear, talking and playing cards or resting quietly. Kiril wrote in a bound notebook he had bought from the ship's purser, who had a surplus of ledgers and logs. His entries were generally short, but this morning he was prolix. He stopped occasionally to put his pencil to the tip of his lower lip and reread his entry. He frowned. Then he set pencil to paper again and continued his pinched scrawl.

"How did you ever become a scrittori with handwriting like that?" Bar-Woten asked. Kiril looked up with a start at the Ibisian standing beside him and scowled fiercely.

"I'd like some privacy," he said, closing the book with a slap and putting the pencil behind his ear under a lock of hair. The Ibisian shrugged and started to walk away. Kiril looked distinctly miserable, then called for him. "I'm sorry," he said. "Come back and sit down." He patted the deck across from where he squatted. Bar-Woten returned just as stoically as he had left and sat. "We shouldn't fight all the time," Kiril said.

"No need for it," Bar-Woten agreed. "Not today, at least. We've chosen our fate."

"How's that?"

"We're going to run for it and follow the fog."

"How?"

"It will break with the wind and the wind is going south today, very gentle. We'll weigh anchor when we can see more to the north than to the south. The captain knows we have a clear channel directly east. We'll sound and follow the currents."

"But the submarine can see us whether there's fog or not."

"I don't see how," Bar-Woten said. "Water's silty."

"It must have some way. These ships don't sound as they sail; they just move."

"The submarine isn't here today anyway, unless it moved in during the night, and nobody heard anything. When the sub moves you can hear it in the hull."

Kiril shook his head dubiously and leaned against the back of a vent. "We won't get away that easily."

"We'll see."

They never had a chance to try their plan. Before the fog lifted the submarine was heard on the surface. When the fog thinned they saw two ships-on-legs moving too slowly to show their foils. Clusters of men in dark uniforms stood on the decks. A bull horn was brought out, and one of the men in black hailed the *Trident*.

"Captain Prekari!"

The captain came forward and answered the call.

"I am Vice-Admiral Gyorgi Lassfal, in command of Ocean Restoration. I was formerly in command of the Weggismarche Merchant Navy. Do you recognize my voice?"

Prekari, standing on the wing of the bridge, answered that he did not — further identification would be necessary. An exchange of personal pleasantries followed, which left no doubt in Prekari's mind that he was talking to his bureaucratic superior. He passed the word along the deck.

"Captain, I have been invited here to tell you there is no

danger. These men wish us no harm. In fact, they want our help in the Restoration. Am I allowed to board your ship and explain these things to you?"

Prekari told him he could come aboard alone.

The vice-admiral was brought to the lowered gangway by a small motor-launch. He came aboard without ceremony and was ushered quickly into Prekari's stateroom. There was nothing left to do on deck but watch the rising fog and examine the near ships more closely.

By midday the vice-admiral left the *Trident*, and Prekari came back to the quarterdeck. He stood on the boat platform to tell them what had been decided.

"Weggismarche, Pallasta, and Nin are now under control of Northerners," he began. He cleared his throat and leaned on a davit. Bar-Woten thought of the day they had first met him, stomping along the deck to his cabin; now he looked tired and weak, half the man he had been. "That is, they are under the care of these people . . . who have lived in peace for many hundreds of years. The weapons and ships, they say, are defensive, used only when exploring in dangerous waters. I believe that story is true on the whole. So does Vice-Admiral Lassfal. They've come south to see what aid they can give to our country.

"They are building emergency shelters for the survivors. The factories we passed are for that purpose. The admiral claims they were brought here piece by piece in the last few weeks. They have ships much larger than any of ours. There are only five or six million people left in our country, a few more in the lands south. Most were killed when the Obelisk fell. All of our cities have been destroyed. The weather has changed. The crops are all gone of course, and so is our livelihood. It sounds as if they might be benevolent, but I think they have other motives. Not unreasonable motives,

146

mind you, but ulterior nonetheless. They have come to read the Obelisk. They have requested our help in digging out the buried portions — as much as possible — and reading and deciphering. The admiral tells me this is a monumental task, enough to fill decades, perhaps centuries. In that time the Northerners will support us, help rebuild, reestablish our economy — apparently making the Obelisk the center of all business and trade. They seem to be decent people — strong-willed, but not unreasonable. They have certain moral strictures we are requested to abide by. These will be outlined at a later date. There is nothing that should be repugnant to us. . . . " He didn't sound completely convinced. Kiril frowned. The captain's message seemed one of defeat — defeat without war, without even preliminary defiance.

"The Obelisk is a thousand kilometers long. Until now, we've never had a chance to read more than a few kilometers of its surface. We've known that the history of the Firstborn extended far higher, with knowledge we could never hope to attain by ourselves. We are now offered the chance." He added in a lower voice, "But at what a cost!" The crew of the *Trident* was deathly still. The fog was gone now. They could smell the smoke from the factories.

"We have nothing else to do. We can't trade our cargo, we can't buy necessary materials and parts, we can't leave the Pale Seas and survive for long with our hearts cut out of us. We have to regrow our hearts here, by giving up the sea, if need be, or working in whatever way we can with this ship to help rebuild Weggismarche. Of this I am convinced. Are you convinced with me?"

The crew said nothing. Then, as if by one motion, they looked over the starboard side to the rugged and denuded land and agreed in a low rumble. Kiril spoke with them, and

Barthel nodded with a catch in his throat, mixed fear and sorrow.

Bar-Woten stood silent with his one eye fixed on Prekari and his lips set. It would soon be time to begin the third leg of their journey.

Nineteen

From the top of Barometer Mountain, two kilometers above the barren plains that stretched to the Pale Seas, the long, geometric bulk of the Obelisk could be seen for at least four hundred kilometers. At the horizon, half of its bulk was buried in the rock and soil of Hegira. Closer than that, the curve of the planet slacked away from the spire until its end spanned the isthmus of Weggismarche and wedged into another mountain four kilometers from Barometer.

Kiril looked down the southern slope and saw the base camp of the surveying party from the *Trident*, and in the bay beyond, the *Trident* herself, tiny as a toy in a puddle. He turned his eyes skyward and shielded them. The light that had replaced the Obelisk's glow was at its noontime peak. Clouds drifted in patches across its concentrated center, casting broad shadows over Barometer and the bay. Bar-Woten climbed slowly and deliberately over the rock pile that edged the northern slope of the peak, and joined Kiril. Barthel wasn't far behind.

"I'm beginning to piece together this stuff about the Wall of the World," Bar-Woten said, regaining his breath with even, deep inhalations. "It's five thousand kilometers from here, to the north, which explains why there are no more Obelisks visible no matter how far north you travel. From what I understand, the Wall itself gives off a glow at the top. There may be smaller Obelisks there or normal ones just beyond it."

"How tall is it?" Kiril asked. Barthel stood beside them and leaned on his climbing pick, his face red and sweaty.

"At least as tall as an Obelisk."

Kiril looked down the northern slope and saw a helicopter landing on a broad rock outcrop, like a bee setting down on a stony gray flower. "Is it true there's writing on the Wall, too?"

"They say so. Because it starts at a forty-two-degree angle, they can climb up its face easier than any of us could scale an Obelisk. That's why they know more than we do. But they can't go higher than a hundred kilometers. The slope increases beyond that, and there's not enough air — not for a man or his machines anyway."

Kiril tried to picture the civilizations along the Wall developing faster, learning faster, trying to spread their culture and knowledge farther south. How long ago had they reached the point where they could learn about submarines, hydrofoils, airplanes, and helicopters in sufficient detail to build them? A few centuries? How long after that before they could build rockets and read even more of the writing higher up? His past few weeks of education still stunned him.

There were huge factories farther north, whose only purpose was to create artificial petroleum products, following a formula on the Wall of the World. There was no natural petroleum on Hegira, as most half-civilized people had learned long ago. Some — such as those in Weggismarche and Pallasta, and even in Mediweva and Ibis — had developed efficient methane engines and made do with that. Those near the Wall, having access to more complicated instructions and designs and the method of making artificial petroleum from waste products, built their factories and developed engines with far more power, and also far more waste.

They had radio communication and were developing the transmission of moving pictures. They had basic rockets, though nowhere near as large as the one in the chasm south of Ubidharm. They had advanced medical knowledge. In all ways they were ahead of their southern neighbors. Yet they had been blocked by solid bands of ignorance, tribes and cities and countryside populations intent on stopping them from spreading Unholy Knowledge any farther. The People of the Wall had had to pass their information across the cultural interfaces gradually — over three hundred years' time — bringing their neighbors into their own fold. But even the People of the Wall had limitations — which began one hundred kilometers from the surface of Hegira.

Now with the fallen Obelisk there were no limitations. In a few decades they would be able to piece together the entire history, culture, and technology of all the civilizations of the First-born.

Kiril almost wished he could stay and learn. But it was too late to stop. The three had to pass beyond the Wall. It was a dead certainty that what lay beyond the Wall was the Land Where Night Is a River. He ran his hand across his forehead and smiled. It was like being halfway through a stormy day riding a scrittori balloon, with clouds beginning to clear.

But they still had a long way to go.

"If we can't climb the thing, how do we get across?" he asked.

"I've been listening to their stories," Bar-Woten said. "Their legends seem to fit those of my country, end to end, completing the stories and adding more details. But they've also seen them — "

"Seen what?" Kiril asked.

"The holes. Every few kilometers there's a hole, about eight kilometers above the base of the wall." He was ebullient. He clasped his hands together and touched two fingers to his beard, smiling broadly as he looked across the plain. "They say when a man is worthy he can go into the hole and walk as far as he pleases . . . right across to the Land Where Night Is a River. Usually the holes are blocked — but for the worthy man they'll open right up!"

"And after that?"

"We'll see soon enough."

"Are they going to let us go north?"

"I don't know. We can only ask."

"They won't believe us."

"Probably not," Bar-Woten agreed. "So we don't tell them you're really a prince." He grinned. "We tell them you're a curious scrittori from a land they've never heard of, and we," he pointed to Barthel and himself, "are your humble student assistants. We've come to the ends of the world to see what there is to see and exchange what we have to give."

"You're hopelessly optimistic."

"These people have no reason to fight. No reason to conquer. They have everything already." He grinned. His guard's down, Kiril thought.

"I never thought an old soldier would trust anybody," he said.

"Nor I. That's why I left."

"The Bey trusts these Wall people?" Barthel asked.

"They could have killed us a dozen times over, and instead they ask us to join their work crews and help them to restore a land they've never visited before."

"Maybe they're ambitious to a fault," Kiril suggested.

"What about the ship in Mur-es-Werd that was damaged by a hydrofoil?" Barthel asked.

"Ah!" Bar-Woten raised his hand. "One unanswered question. Maybe they fired first."

"Perhaps there's more than one civilization with technology like this," Kiril said. "What's going to happen when they all meet?"

"I don't know," Bar-Woten said. He stroked his beard, then looked at Kiril as if the Mediwevan had pricked some happy private balloon and brought them all down hard. Kiril was surprised by the look — he'd made the suggestion almost cheerfully. But he sobered and said, "That's the way it always is: two equals meet, and they have to fight."

"There is a reason for everything," Barthel said. "Allah dropped the Obelisk here to stop such squabbles. He dropped it in a land of good people perhaps."

"No, no," Bar-Woten mused. "Barthel, would your Allah sacrifice ninety million people to hand good cards and fair dice to someone else?"

Barthel frowned for a moment, then nodded, yes. "It would not be without precedent," he said. "My Allah is no simple God, Bey."

"I opt for letting the Fall remain a mystery until we hear a better explanation not based on faith," Kiril said. "There are things faith is good for, and this isn't one of them."

They scrambled down the southern slope toward the camp. A work party of fifty men and women were laying tarmac for an airfield a half kilometer from the beach. By the time the three had descended, a whistle blew for dinner, and all work stopped.

A communal dining tent had been erected, and dinner was served inside with kerosene lamps on the tables. Most of the crew of the *Trident* ate under the canvas, and about thirty People of the Wall, including the camp director. He was a grinning, gray-haired man, tall and slightly stoop-shouldered, who called himself Orshist. After the meal was finished he went to a small platform at one end of the tent and set up a board to outline the plans for the excavation of the Obelisk.

His manner was crisp and brief. He carried a collapsible pointer and used it to emphasize his words like a fencer executing a riposte.

"We have the spire," he said, "and we have Hegira. Hegira in this region has four layers that are familiar to us. They begin with topsoil, which is sparse here, and overburden, which consists of dead dirt and broken rock. Beneath that is the groundwater layer, which extends for at least a kilometer, and beneath that is plastic mantle. The spire has buried itself some four hundred kilometers from here, deep into the groundwater layer. Beyond that, at its midpoint, it has broken through this layer and struck mantle. But of primary interest is where it has lodged in the mountains. The mountains, contrary to what we've learned of geology on Earth, did not form because of drifting continents, of which Hegira has none. The mountains have always been here. Where the spire has fallen across mountains, it has broken through four layers and found a fifth. This fifth is not another extension of mantle, but something quite different. It's porous like a honeycomb, made from what we now think is primary vulcanism — which could only have happened at Hegira's formation. Some of the pores are big enough for a man to step into."

Kirl and Barthel listened attentively, but Bar-Woten was mulling something over, his bearded chin resting in his hand. His eye was closed.

"If we wish to uncover the spire completely we must dig away all these layers where they cover the sides. We may never know all of the text on the underside, but fortunately the spire is unlike the Wall, and each side supports its own text instead of a continuation from side to side."

Bar-Woten opened his eye and thought of the honeycomb material, pores big enough to hold a man. That seemed very important, because it reminded him of the rind of a fruit

154

they had eaten in Golumbine, called *sati*. It had a thin, tough outer shell under which was an equally tough but spongy and resilient white layer, like tree rubber. The white layer had been porous and dry.

Orshist went into detail about the excavations and produced a chart that showed where the first readings would be made.

"We have a pretty good idea of the history of the Firstborn to the middle of the twentieth centure *anno Domini*," he said, pointing to the end of the Obelisk. "Information here could already give us a lifetime of study and development, since we come across complicated philosophies, whole new brands of physical science, and vast, important literatures. But now we need to know how we are related to the First-born and what sort of world Hegira is. With this knowledge we might begin to find some meaning in our existence."

Bar-Woten, like a weather vane, showed by the set of his mouth and the angle of his eyelid what he thought of Orshist's words. He didn't move a muscle otherwise. He reminded Kiril of a cat intent on its spring.

"So we'll begin in areas we can interpret. That will put us at this point, two hundred kilometers from the base. We'll also record at the very top of the spire, near the dormant sun source, but we won't begin direct interpretation. The language appears to be incomprehensible, even in the standard phonetic script of the spire. Numbers play a large part in the language toward that end. In short, we are about to study the entire history and accomplishment of the First-born, perhaps up to the time they performed that unknown act, or had an unknown act performed upon them, and produced ourselves, the Second-born.

"Work crews will assemble tomorrow morning. Committees and working unions for the distribution of supplies and living quarters will meet and organize at each camp. Factories will be set up along the coast for the construction of roads, the rebuilding of cities, the manufacture of digging machines, and the processing of raw materials. We begin a job worthy of any civilization on Hegira!"

Kiril fidgeted. He could hardly remember what Elena looked like now, and yet he was still obligated — almost against his will — to push on with Bar-Woten and Barthel. He would rather have stayed and helped in the interpretation, in the learning and deciphering and recording, for the spirit of the thing was in his blood, and future adventure in unknown lands seemed far less attractive. His fists clenched, and he couldn't separate the confused strings of thought in his head.

Twenty

"Kiril! Wake up!"

The Mediwevan fought out of his slumber and had the familiar sensation of not remembering where he was. The tent canvas overhead and the thin-padded cot, which had become as unyielding as stone during the night, had been forgotten in sleep, and now he didn't know what they were. Barthel came into the tent through the flap, stumbled over a roll of clothing, and grabbed him by the shoulder. Kiril rubbed his sleep-smeared eyes and asked what was going on.

"They arrested the Bey!"

"Who?" he asked, still foggy.

"The Bey! They've put Bar-Woten in jail!"

"Why would they do that?" he asked peevishly.

"I think," Barthel began, then lowered his voice, for others in the tent were waking, "I think he asked a woman to make love to him — solicitation, is that the word here? He was reported to some officials of the People of the Wall, and they put him in jail."

"Kristos," Kiril said, rolling his legs off the cot and plopping his bare feet onto the hard-packed dirt floor. It was cold. He searched hurriedly for his shoes.

"We should go to the captain," Barthel said. "He is our representative until the new union leaders are voted for."

"I don't know," Kiril murmured, tying up his laces. He saw then that he didn't have his pants on, and it took him twice as long to slip the legs over his shoes and buckle the catch. He searched in the early morning grayness for his shirt and found it in the dirt, where Barthel's feet had kicked it off the roll.

The morning air was foggy and dismal. They walked across the rocky ground to the Administration Tent. No one was there yet, and the empty fold-out tables and chairs mocked them. The tent canvas flapped softly in the breeze. "Where's the jail?" Kiril asked. Barthel nodded and walked ahead of him across the fresh tarmac to the opposite end of the airfield, near the beach.

The jail was a wooden compound, which until now had been virtually empty. It was built of driftwood, scrap lumber, and tar paper and wasn't exceptionally strong, but its symbolism was still impressive. It was an ugly hodge-podge of a building.

There was only one guard. He looked them over sleepily and then let them in. Bar-Woten was in a tiny cell faced with heavy iron-barred doors. He was wide awake and apparently hadn't slept all night. His face was an empty mask.

Kiril walked back and forth in front of the bars for a minute, fuming. "How in *hell* did you manage this?" he finally asked. Bar-Woten shook his head.

"I don't know," he said. "They're of your kind, not mine, I suspect. I had no idea a compliment to a woman was a crime."

"What an asinine thing to — " But Kiril cut himself off, looking at the jailer, and sat down on a small stool. Barthel remained standing, shifting from one foot to another. "What are we going to do?"

"Well," said Bar-Woten, switching abruptly from Teutan to Mediwevan, "we could take this as a warning and get the hell out of here, head north."

"What a mess that would land us in. How could we survive in this country?"

"You seemed anxious to try it a few weeks ago. It's either that or stand trial for something I'm obviously guilty of, with witnesses" — Kiril groaned — "and that would probably get me a year or so in prison. That's what this fine gentleman says," Bar-Woten grumbled, pointing to the jailer.

Kiril stood and told Bar-Woten they'd talk to Prekari. The Ibisian wasn't encouraged. "Listen," he said. "I sounded these people pretty carefully last night while I was being arrested. They have one fault, and it's similar to your own — they're self-righteous and highly moral on affairs of the flesh. They're peaceful and prosperous. They're also convinced they can fairly apply their law to all. Try overcoming that with the captain."

Kiril and Barthel left the jail and walked across the tarmac to the administration tent. There was activity inside — two young boys from the *Trident* stood by the awning entrance with arms folded, radiating dignity, guardians of the ship's mates and the captain talking at a table within. Kiril and Barthel challenged the boys' bluff by walking by quickly and not saying a word until they were at the table. The captain stood up, tired and worn, and asked them what they wanted. Kiril told him what had happened.

"Serves the man right. Doesn't he have enough sense to be discreet?"

"I do not think discretion has much to do with it, sir," Barthel said. "I could have fallen into the same trouble. Any of your crew. Can we let him stand trial for a law we didn't know about?"

"It's a difficult problem," said a woman's voice from across the tent. It was Avra, sitting in a corner near the entrance with stacks of paper on a table before her. A shaft of light from a chink in the roof played about her hands, moving with the rippling of the tent fabric. Her face was dark and ghostly. She reminded Kiril of a Norn, and he felt a chill.

"What can we do about it?" he asked.

"Probably nothing. It's a minor charge and won't net him much of a sentence. He'll probably be taken to the settlement at the fifty-kilometer mark on the Obelisk, stand trial, and spend two or three months clearing dirt with the labor gangs. He can stand it."

Barthel spoke up, his voice surprisingly sharp, considering he was addressing Avra. "The Bey will not be locked up."

"He'll have to face it," Avra said tersely.

"You don't understand. He will kill somebody before that happens."

"Is he that stupid?" the captain asked.

Barthel pounded the table with his fist. His face was dark, and his eyes seemed clouded by smoke. "No one says the Bey is stupid!" he rasped. He turned and left the tent. Kiril stayed behind, uncertain what to do or how to interpret the scene. He felt he should apologize, but now he was angry, too. It seemed a ridiculous hindrance after they'd traveled so many thousands of kilometers and faced so much danger.

"We're their guests," Avra said. "We have difficult diplomacies to work out with them, and very little to bargain with."

"The captain told us they were reasonable and helpful," Kiril said. "But all I see is smoke pouring into the Pale Seas and crews being set up to dig out the Obelisk. Now they slap us in the face with this ludicrous charge. I sense a darker motive."

The room was silent.

"No one behaves this way without a reason," Kiril added when the silence had lengthened.

"I think Barthel is right," he concluded, and he turned briskly to leave.

"All well, all good," Bar-Woten told them when they visited his cell for the second time. He hadn't moved. His body was charged with an electric tension. The guard — a man about Kiril's age — was pale and noticeably reluctant to stay in the building with him. Again they spoke in Mediwevan, but for a few moments Bar-Woten and Barthel conversed in Arbuck, which Kiril understood only slightly.

Then they left, and Barthel was quiet.

The day seemed unbearably long. Survey crews climbed Barometer and continued their measuring, but Kiril wasn't among them. He stood by the landing strip waiting for the plane to arrive, knowing it came this time to take Bar-Woten to his trial. He waited until dusk, walking to the food shed and mess tent after sunset to eat, then to the beach to listen to the swift surge of the river heading seaward.

The airplane didn't arrive by late evening, and the landing field, without lights as yet, was closed. Kiril went to his cabin to try for a few hours of sleep.

He didn't have a chance. He was caught between slumber and nervous alertness when Barthel called from outside the tent. The other sleepers grumbled, and one sat up in the murky light of the pole lamp rubbing his eyes. Kiril motioned for him to go back to sleep and held his fingers to his lips. Then he swung out of the cot, automatically picked up the clothes he had packed earlier, and left the tent.

A flaring gas flame provided a guttering illumination across the end of the camp, exaggerating the shadows and emphasizing the frequent gusts of wind. The night was dark and without bright fire doves. Barthel stood next to a barrel covered by a wire screen. Someone else was behind him, shadowy and indistinct, but Kiril knew who it was. "How did he get out?"

"Never mind that," Bar-Woten said from the darkness. Barthel took Kiril's arm and pulled him along.

They crossed the tarmac. Rocky and molten terrain began several hundred meters north of the camp. Bar-Woten told them they would follow the beach for a while, then duck into the stony maze if they were pursued.

"I thought there weren't supposed to be night landings," Barthel said. He stopped in the dark, squinting eastward at the pair of red lights racing low over the water. "They can't land on the runway. No lights."

"That's not an airplane," Kiril said. "It might be a helicopter. It's flying too low and too slow to be an — "

Bar-Woten grabbed both of them by the arms. "Quickly!" he said. "Into the rocks."

"Why?" Kiril asked, resisting the rush. "No one's after us."

"Trust a soldier's instincts for once! Into the rocks."

They broke into a run. Engines roared from the east. Bright lights split the camp into scattered spots of day. Barthel stumbled on a rock and split his knee open. Limping and gasping, he held up his hands, and they lifted him to cover behind the rocks. Kiril peered over a split boulder. The base camp was alive with running, shouting people.

"What's going on?" he asked wonderingly.

"They're being attacked," Bar-Woten said.

"Nobody's shooting — "

Gouts of flame billowed from the main tents. A vivid red arrow of light swept the camp. Everything it touched flared incandescent.

"They're ships," Bar-Woten said. "But they're going faster than the hydrofoils — they're flying above the water!"

At least five of the craft skimmed up the beach, each shooting lethal red beams into the camp. The ships resembled broad scrub brushes scouring the water. They danced on wide fringes of rubber and threw plumes of spray behind them. Each was fifty or sixty meters long, rounded and streamlined. They didn't slow as they approached the beach.

Bar-Woten examined the Khemite's leg by matchlight. He tore a strip from the bottom of his shirt and tied a bandage. "It's only a cut," he said. "Hold your leg out straight."

"What are they doing up there? I can't see anything." Barthel gritted his teeth.

"They're killing everybody."

"Who? With what?"

"I don't know. Just be glad you're here."

"They're coming up on the beach!" Kiril said. "They can go anywhere!"

"What are they shooting with?" Barthel asked.

"I don't know," Bar-Woten said. "Keep still."

"We have to leave, or they'll kill us too!" The Khemite groaned in pain.

"We're well hidden."

"They'll come after us," Kiril agreed. "God, I can't stand it!" he held his hands up to his ears. "It's slaughter!" He crouched to jump down from the ledge.

Something blinding flashed over them. His hair caught fire, and for an instant, amazed, he stood like a torch. Bar-Woten reached up and pulled him off the rock, smothering his head in a coat. When he removed the coat, the Mediwevan was unconscious. His scalp hadn't been burned, but the smell of his singed hair added to the sickening smoke drifting across the rocks. Barthel's glancing eyes picked up stray gleams in the orange half-light. He struggled up from Bar-Woten's grip to look across the airfield. "Holy Allah!" he said, ducking down quickly. He grimaced as his knee flexed.

"Keep the leg straight!" Bar-Woten commanded.

"We can't stay here. We have to go farther away, or they'll kill us."

"You speak without thinking — " The Ibisian pulled his

163

head in like a turtle as another beam flashed above them. "They've got the wrath of Samhain at work out there. They'll scythe us if we stick our heads up. Best to stay here for a moment."

There were fewer screams now. Scattered shots punctuated the crackle and hiss of burning. The engines of the craft throttled and hummed. Kiril came to and reached for his scalp. He brushed his hair vigorously with his fingers. They came away smudged. "Am I burned?" he asked.

"Not badly. You're lucky, young friend," Bar-Woten said. His face was fixed into a death's-head smile. Barthel leaned back in the shadow of the ledge and muttered prayers with his hands clasped. Kiril wondered why he wasn't praying himself. Mediweva's provincial God didn't seem to have any jurisdiction here. He brushed the singed hairs from his head.

"What are we going to do?"

"Wait," Bar-Woten said. He stood up and put his knees on the ledge, barely raising his head over the rim of the rock. "There are men leaving the ships. They're carrying weapons — guns, I think. Some of the camp people are surrendering. They aren't shooting."

"Taking prisoners?" Barthel asked.

"It would seem so." He ducked back. "We'll lie low and creep around these rocks as fast as we can. Nobody is close."

"Who are they?" Kiril asked.

The Ibisian shrugged. "The rivals are here. Do you think a bone as big as an Obelisk wouldn't draw every jackal in the area? The real story's barely begun now."

"Allah was good to us, having you arrested," Barthel said. "There is a reason for everything."

Bar-Woten grunted. "Let's go."

"Morning in an hour or so," Kiril said as they crawled over the rough, pebbly ground between the bigger boulders. "We should be pretty far from here by then."

An ear-pounding *whumpf* broke the quiet behind them. Bar-Woten stood up and saw the *Trident*'s fragments riding a flower of smoke and fire. Bits of blazing wood fell on the beach, forcing ranks of prisoners to break and run. "It's the ship," he said. "I don't think the new ones did it, though."

"Did what?"

"She's gone."

They continued to crawl.

"Stop!"

Kiril looked up. A shadow on the rock above them pointed a gun into the crevice.

"Come out of there, all of you," the shadow said.

"What does he want?" Bar-Woten asked.

"He wants us to get up out of here," Kiril replied. "He's speaking English — good old English. That," he grimaced, "was my specialty a few years ago." He held up his hands, and the others mimicked him. "Coming," he said.

"Damn right you are. Nothing false, now."

A boat rowed silently near the water-washed rocks. It was filled with men dressed in black, all sporting wicked-looking rifles.

"Into the water," the man said. "It's shallow. Go on."

They were hauled into the boat and securely tied with scratchy ropes. Bound and helpless, they were pitched into the bottom. A shadow stood over them, bending and reaching out to examine them. The shadow's profile was irregular. A flap of black cloak fell away and Barthel looked directly into the figure's face. His skin paled in the lamplight from the prow. Kiril lay face down in the boat and couldn't see.

"It's not a man," the Khemite whispered.

"Be gentle with these," the figure said, it's voice muffled. "They're different from the others."

The oars were pulled in, and the boat drifted with the river currents.

Twenty-one

Kiril looked their captors over quickly as they were shoved into line with the rest of the prisoners. The night hid the features of the one Barthel had said wasn't a man. It walked to the rear of the armed guards and whispered instructions to several uniformed men. It moved its limbs with an odd jerking motion. Its loose-fitting robes formed novel humps and hollows as the wind grabbed at it.

Those tents that hadn't burned were being searched. Sporadic gunfire still accented the wind. The hulking flying ships whistled and hummed. A ramp was lowered from the nearest craft, and the first line of thirty prisoners was herded into a dark aft compartment, Kiril among them. Barthel and Bar-Woten were in the next line but didn't come aboard his craft.

The cramped quarters reeked with fear. A few lights flickered on above them, strips of white in the low ceiling, and he saw the floor was padded. Seats lined the walls. Those who could sit did so. Nobody from the *Trident* was in the group beside Kiril. He squatted on the padding and rubbed his face with his hands. His fingers came away wet with tears. He felt like dying, he was so confused.

The engines beneath them coughed, seemed to laugh, then broke into a body-strumming roar. The craft lurched and rose. The engines pitched higher.

Sometime in the next few hours he slept. He awoke in a press of bodies and struggled free of nightmares about slaughter. Most of the captives were breathing slowly, rhythmically, a sea of flesh gently rolling. He wiped sleep from his eyes and wet his finger to erase traces of dried tears from his cheeks. A few owlish eyes returned his gaze from across the room, but most of the prisoners were lost in blind, escapeful slumber.

He had to urinate. The pressure was almost unbearable. He crossed his legs and gritted his teeth to still the insistent acid pangs. There was already urine smell in the air from others. He felt a small, mild nausea, a reminder he still had a stomach and that he hadn't eaten for a while. At least the flying ship didn't roll with the water — if they were still over water.

He stood without disturbing those sprawled around him, stretched his arms, and tensed his leg muscles. He could touch the ceiling. With one finger he felt a light-strip. It was warm but not hot. He thought of Barthel and Bar-Woten. Perhaps they were dead already, and he was on his own. He found that hard to accept. He had gotten so much strength from the two despite their differences.

"We've been moving for six hours," said a man across the cabin. Kiril recognized the guard of the makeshift jail. He had a broad bruise above his eye, and he held one arm as if it were a baby. "Did your friends get away?"

Kiril shook his head. Unsettled, he looked away from the guard. "Your friends didn't hurt me badly," the man said. "But these bastards — I think they've broken my arm."

He didn't seem to hold a grudge, but Kiril thought it best to consider everyone and everything an enemy now. He felt it was within his power to kill if he had to — something he had never known before. He flexed his hands and looked at them speculatively.

If Bar-Woten and Barthel were dead he'd have to protect

himself. He was no longer a ward, an amateur. He was a caged animal.

The engines changed pitch. The craft banked forward, then rocked back. He tumbled over as they slowed.

The other prisoners were waking. Questions passed back and forth in volleys. A man and a woman hugged each other joyfully, then gazed around like cornered rabbits.

The engines stopped. The craft thumped gently to rest. The hatch opened and blinding daylight poured in, silhouetting five armed guards. The prisoners were herded from the craft down the ramp, stepping into soft snow covering gray concrete. Slate-gray mountains rose on three sides, and on the fourth a stretch of wave-flaked water. Above was a bank of rushing clouds, piling around the mountains and sculpting wind-saucers in their lee. Kiril's heart leaped with the crisp smell of the air — forests and cold stretches of beach, lakewater smell, rain smell. The land was horrible and beautiful at the same time, mountains raw with black jagged rock and stunted trees, the wind like a flight of icicles. The prisoners beat themselves with their arms and puffed their cheeks out, huffing, trying to keep warm. The guards kept their slender guns raised and ready.

The thirty were lined up on the concrete and snow in two rows and made to stand until they were blue.

A second craft climbed from the water of the lake and whisked across the concrete apron to park beside the first. A third followed, and both disgorged loads of prisoners. These were lined up twenty meters behind Kiril's row. He craned his neck searching for Bar-Woten and Barthel. He thought he saw the Khemite, but couldn't be sure. He was afraid to turn. His teeth chattered until they threatened to vibrate his aching eyes out. His ears were numb, and when he touched his armpit-warmed fingers to them, they tingled.

Trucks with canvas-covered beds rolled onto the strip and

stood with engines idling, white smoke belching from pipes hung near the cabs. Kiril saw the shrouded figure climb down a ladder from the second hovercraft. It wore a silvery mask beneath its dark hood. Two men conferred with it, then took its arms and led it to the cab of the truck. It tugged them to a stop and turned to point to the ranks of prisoners. Its hand, Kiril saw, was gloved. Beneath the silvery mesh of the glove there could only have been three fingers, unless more than one digit occupied each finger. He felt a tremor pass through him that was more than just cold. Where could such a thing have come from? Perhaps, he consoled himself, it was only a man made up to look strange to cow the captives. But its walk was so authentically different that he doubted it was human.

The guards prodded the captives with their guns and marched them into the backs of the trucks. There in the windy canvas tunnels they sat until the gates were closed and the trucks lurched head. Then they rushed to peer between the truck panels and the canvas.

Kiril found a position where he could see the concrete landing field pass beneath them, changing to a rocky, ice-pocketed road.

"We're being guarded from the cab," word passed. "They have guns aimed at us."

"Maybe we can slip out the rear," a woman suggested. She stood up to see if the folds of canvas above the gate were tied down, but was wrenched back into her seat by a sudden bump.

"We're going too fast," a man said. "We'd be killed."

"We're going to be killed anyway," the jail guard said. "You know who these people are? They're from the *east* . . ." He said the word as if it were synonymous with evil.

"We don't know that yet," another said.

"Who else could build machines like these but the ones who've been dropping rockets on the Library Cities?"

"There may be others, but even so, they're all trying to destroy us," the woman near the gate spoke up. "We have to get away from them and fight!"

Kiril listened with interest. "Two equals," he murmured to himself. "They have to fight it out."

But it wasn't only their fight. With instruments like the fire guns and flying ships it wouldn't be long before everyone on Hegira would face a rout. It would be Bar-Woten's March all over again — but this time the Ibisians would look like reckless children.

He remembered the Bible and thought of Cain and Abel. Cain meant "smithy," or forger of tools. The tool-forger slew his farmer brother because God looked on the brother's sacrifice with more favor. Now in a different place and far different time, those with the better tools won — just as the tiger with the swifter claws gained dominance in the forest. Mercy, kindness, grace, and beauty had nothing to do with human existence in such crazed times. He shook his head. He was so far from all of it, so isolated in mind and temper — yet he dearly wished, with a portion of his darker soul, that he had the finest tools of all. He would scourge his way to the Wall like a tide of cats through a mouse village — a tide of stray cats. All the stray cats were licking at him, testing him with claws, pulling away the pieces of soggy paper he had wrapped around himself for warmth. They mewed and purred and rubbed against him —

He lifted his head up and wrapped his arms around himself to stop his shivering. He was freezing — they all were. More and more quiet, eyes glazed, faces blue, lips purple. The truck jolted to a stop.

Hardly aware where he was going, Kiril followed the stumbling crowd of prisoners down a sloping ramp into a concrete corridor. The guards jostled the slow ones until they regained their footing and lurched after. Kiril's feet were numb.

But it was warm! Warm air flowed up to meet them as an inner door opened, and they leaned into the revivifying breeze as if it were life itself. Moaning, crying and grunting with pain, they were pushed into a narrow, gray-green waiting room. Kiril felt his pants crackle, then go damp. He had urinated, and the urine had frozen on his trouser legs. He didn't care.

He thumped himself and grinned and kicked his legs out, as the others did. But in a few minutes their joy turned to misery. Their limbs began to thaw, and with each inroad of warmth a rigid needle poked at their bones. Then their muscles cramped and they cried out in agony.

Other prisoners followed. Barthel came through the door, his face haggard and pale olive, and behind him a man with a patch over one eye — Bar-Woten. They were both alive! Kiril felt like shouting at them, but his tongue tripped up his words. He was filled with a deadly thirst.

He had never been more miserable in all his life. But each little addition of misery, which in itself would have made him weak and ill, seemed to diminish the total. He seemed to draw strength from his pain and discomfort.

The groups weren't allowed to mingle. They were pushed up against the opposite walls and told to flatten themselves or lose their legs. Iron bars swung from the ceiling and enclosed them, giving just enough room to stand flat to the wall. They could only look across at their caged companions. Bar-Woten reached his hand out to Kiril and feebly gestured. A guard butted it with his rifle.

Hoses sprayed lukewarm water on them. The air was filled with fog as the water struck the cold walls. Blood, dirt, urine, and feces washed from the prisoners and whirled away down the drains in the middle of the room.

Kiril guessed there were about a hundred of them. They were shivering again in the wet and screaming with the pain of their thaw. Kiril suddenly found himself elevated to a level of calm detachment. He looked on the prisoners and their captors and saw only silly, inconsequential animals. Then what was he? Another animal, temporarily jolted above concern with his body, perhaps to share some higher sense of humor. They all looked ridiculous — playacting amateur roles conjured by ridiculously limited talents.

Could he think of anything better? No, he admitted. He was no better. Just less blind.

A second spray, pungent with disinfectant, was directed over them. Fans and radiant heaters were brought in from another door. The heaters were turned on, then the fans.

When it was over a third of them were dead. Kiril dragged himself out of a swimming haze and looked at the middle of the room. The cloaked figure stood talking to a uniformed man. The man's face held a mixture of obedience and repugnance. The ends of his mouth curled downward in a half-sneer, half-snarl. He said something Kiril couldn't hear.

The figure gestured with a draped arm, and the fans and heaters were carried out. The officer walked before the opposite row of prisoners, glancing diffidently at the hanging corpses. He spoke, first in the melodic tongue of the People of the Wall, then in loud, clear Teutan.

"Some of you here may be important to us."

"I am!" a man shouted. "I'll talk about anything!"

The officer's look changed to scorn. "You'll be asked questions. They require specific answers, correct answers." The officer smiled. "If you don't answer correctly, I'll turn you over to this fellow. He's a demon. You've noticed his shape? He comes from hell, not a woman's womb. He'll broil your hearts as if they were on a spit. I hope you understand."

The cloaked figure turned to the wall opposite Kiril and began at one end. Its sibilant voice reached through the sudden quiet like a serpent's hiss.

Kiril struggled to stay awake, but he couldn't. His vision narrowed. He looked at everything through a wind-filled cave, drawing farther back with each second until the rush carried him from the receding light.

"And you?" the voice asked. "You are from very far, too, are you?"

Kiril looked up. He wiped a dribble of saliva from his lower jaw as he stared into the silvery mask. "Elena," he said softly.

"How far away do you live?"

"Mediweva," he answered. "Very far."

"Just a sailor who's traveled far? Or did something compel you to come here?"

"Something," Kiril said. "Elena. Take off your mask."

"What brought you here?"

"You did."

"Not I. Something specific."

Kiril saw Barthel and Bar-Woten standing in the middle of the room under close watch by three guards.

"I had to save you. Save her." He was aware now whom he was talking to.

"Her?"

"My only love." That was hypocritical, he thought. The self-accusation echoed and vanished.

"Ah." The figure gestured.

The cage opened. When he fell, he was caught by yielding arms and taken to join his companions.

"Did you see where we are?" Bar-Woten asked. A guard

shouted at him. He glared back. "We're in the country of the Wall!"

The guard raised his rifle, and Bar-Woten backed off with hands up, placating.

The Wall.

Twenty-two

They sat in the tiny cell and stared listlessly at the padded walls. Bar-Woten crouched with his hands clasped between his knees, knocking his knuckles against his legs. Barthel stood and picked his teeth with a fingernail. They had been given a thick gruel three hours before. It was acting on them unpleasantly. Kiril lay on his back with head and shoulders against a wall, looking green and feeling very docile.

"We've been drugged," Bar-Woten said. Kiril nodded. They wouldn't offer much resistance in their condition. A small window in the door showed them the hall outside, and by peering at an angle they could see the rigid shoulder of a guard, but nothing more.

The door swung open. An officer stepped into the cell and looked down at Kiril. "You are the Mediwevan?" he asked in thickly accented Teutan.

"Speak English. I can understand. Yes, I'm the Mediwevan."

"Come with me," the officer said. He reached down and picked Kiril up. With a last look over his shoulder at his companions he was pulled down the hall to a brightly lit room beyond.

The room was outfitted like a surgery ward, with a central couch covered by worn brown leather and strips of absorbent cotton. He was strapped onto the couch and his pulse and blood pressure were taken. An orange-robed man with intersecting black lines drawn across his bald scalp bent over him with a syringe in hand.

The demon-figure entered from another door. "You may administer," it said. It leaned over Kiril as the needle went into his arm. "This will not hurt you. Just to find out what you are . . . "

Kiril went blank.

He awoke with a sour taste in his mouth and the shock of smelling salts in his nose.

"You've been cooperative," the thing in black told him. He was taken to the cell. Barthel and Bar-Woten were removed next. Kiril asked the guard why they were both going. The guard looked at him sternly, then checked up and down the corridor before answering. "We believe you're the one we want," he said. "But we will test these two just in case." He swung the door shut and locked it.

In two hours the Ibisian and the Khemite were brought back. Bar-Woten weaved a little and slumped to the floor. Barthel stood rigid against the wall, eyes wide and staring into the opposite corner of the cell.

"What did they make me say?" Bar-Woten asked.

"Nothing," Barthel snapped. The Khemite looked into the corner and flinched as if from a blow. What Bar-Woten had revealed under hypnosis was slowly mangling Barthel's insides. He had never suspected. . . .

Overhead they heard the sounds of distant explosions. Kiril peered through the window and saw the guard standing away from the cell, looking anxiously down the hall.

The lights went out. After an hour they slept. Bar-Woten snored loudly, head lolling between his legs. Kiril hung on the edge of sleep. He heard someone move in the cell, but stirred and drifted off.

"No," Barthel said. He closed his eyes but couldn't block out what he saw. In the corner, standing above the reclining

176

Kiril, was Barthel's mother. She glowed faintly like the sea, and her throat opened into a second smiling mouth. What she murmured to him he could not accept. But it was true. He had heard. "Not now," he said.

She spoke to him again.

"No."

He turned away from the corner and butted his head softly against the padding.

The lights came on again. Kiril stood and stretched in the cramped space. Barthel slept on, standing with his head wedged into the corner. Bar-Woten looked at Kiril speculatively from his spot on the floor.

"You're the chosen one," he said. "They're sure you're the one who'll get them into the Wall."

"Get who in?"

"The thin ones. You told the right story, I suppose. Barthel didn't. I'm sure I didn't. The one who isn't human, it spoke to the guard while they were making Barthel talk. It spoke English but I could understand. There are three of them here."

"Three of who?" Kiril asked, mind still foggy from sleep.

"The thin, strange ones. They aren't from this part of Hegira. They came across the Wall in a ship of some sort. They've made a pact, and they're sharing knowledge with the English-speakers."

"They want me to take them to the Wall?"

"You're lucky," Bar-Woten said, nodding. "You'll reach your goal. I doubt if we will."

"I don't want to help them with anything," Kiril said. "They don't deserve it."

"The thin ones might be more friendly than the English-speakers. They didn't like the slaughter at the Obelisk camp. Seemed to think there might have been more like you. Dead pilgrims are no good to them."

"What are the English-speakers doing for them?"

"Didn't say." Bar-Woten's face crinkled into a smile. "It's fairly obvious, though. The thin ones want to get back to where they came from."

"Through the Wall?"

"Any way they can. Perhaps the English-speakers are building them another rocket."

"Then I pity them. They'll be double-crossed."

Bar-Woten shrugged. "I don't understand much of anything now."

Barthel jerked and pulled away from his corner. He rubbed his eyes, then looked over Kiril's shoulder and seemed relieved.

The door opened an hour after they were all awake. Another officer, paunchy and florid, ordered them out of the cell and took them down the hall in the direction opposite the laboratory. Two young, wan-faced guards followed with holstered pistols.

A hovercraft waited on the concrete airstrip. Craters ten and twenty meters across had been punched into the pavement and the surrounding rocky hills. Fragments of metal littered the area.

The fat officer rapped the butt of his gun on the port of the hovercraft. The port swung open, and a ladder came down. "Climb in," he told them. They went up the ladder into the ship. The guards followed, and the officer managed to squeeze through with some straining. A low, round metal tube led them around the circumference to the main cabin. A small barred cell had been welded to the floor and ceiling of the adjacent passenger cubicle. The guards put them in and locked the door behind.

The hovercraft coughed and roared. Somewhere metal screeched across concrete. Then she lurched and rose. The pilot, hidden behind a thick steel shield, took them across the apron and over the lake.

They could get glimpses of their flight only through the edges of the clear canopy that extended beyond the shield. Gray, cragged mountains came toward them as they skirted the perimeter of the lake. The rocks passed away abruptly as the hovercraft made a long, slow turn to the right toward the middle of the lake. Rock walls flashed by on both sides as they passed through a narrow sound.

Barthel stared with determination through the bars at the shield. Bar-Woten sat relaxed with his back wedged into one corner of the cell, studying the slender view of their travel. Kiril alternated between his two companions and the view, trying to puzzle what had happened to all of them.

The trip took an hour. The hovercraft slowed and pulled into a narrow harbor ringed with walls of slate-black stone. It vaulted with a rumble and a slight bump up a ramp of wooden pilings. The guards came alert suddenly and opened the cell on orders from the fat officer. They were led outside.

"We have a special treat," the officer said, slipping the words conspiratorially from the side of his mouth as they walked beside him. "A parade. You should enjoy tomorrow."

Ahead of them lay a solid mass of grayness, as though concentrated storms had packed so thickly they merged without feature. Nearer, clouds broke from the monotony and asserted their own turmoil. Rain fell in wind-blown draperies onto the green, jungle-covered hills and valleys that butted up against the ascending curve of the Wall. Nearer still, obscured by plummets and feathers of mist pouring over the hills, were masses of buildings, angular, like scattered blocks of lead. The sight made Kiril's heart sink. A land of no cheer, no variety . . . it choked the eyes. Yet it had an unmistakable, grave grandeur.

The officer was obviously proud of his city. But he was

also a little cowed, as though the solemnity and monotony were not exactly what he'd expected. Thunder pranced near the gray end of the world. The Wall flashed sheet-white with an eyelike wink — roof of clouds the upper lid, gray-green jungled hills and peaks the lower. The gaze was cold and expectant, like the eye of an *untersay draken*.

"Faster," the officer said. The wind picked up and ruffled their matted hair.

A long, sleek silver train waited for them at the end of the wood ramp. Steam hissed from the engine. The rails made plaintive squeaks. The air smelled of lightning and storm. It tickled Bar-Woten's nose, and he wriggled his face, making his patch bob. He threw a side look at Kiril as he rubbed his nose. Clearer than anything, it told Kiril the Ibisian was worried.

"This car," the officer directed. They climbed into the stepwell, then waited as the inner door opened. More guards waited within, and two of them hooded thin ones. The interior of the car was dark brown suede and chrome steel with a cleanliness that showed rigid care. Two olive-colored tanks of translucent glass were bolted to the floor at the opposite end of the car. The older, tougher guards around these were fully armed. They carried pistols, daggers on their belts, and heavy, brutal rifles stubby as toadstools.

The three were forced to sit in a single seat with prods of elbows and hands on shoulders. The thin aliens stood immobile and silent a few steps from their tanks. Thick fluid lapped in the cylinders. An array of pipes curved from each tank and disappeared into the floor.

The train began to move.

The greater part of the ten-minute ride was spent on a long, fragile-looking trestle that crossed labyrinthine ridges of jungle-covered rock. Rivers crept through the gorges and poured into the lakes farther south, eventually falling into the Pale Seas. The ridges began to look artificially flattened, though still verdant; then buildings occupied them, and finally the land rose in one triumphant, humorless surge to a series of plateaus. The city of the English-speakers sprawled across the tablelands. Closer, the buildings glittered with walls of glass and polished metal. Counterpoints of coppery red and rust lanced up the sides of the taller structures. Monumental cubes were rolled on edge and supported by concrete pillars, faced with glass and steel and something the color of pewter. There were towers, prisms, all sharply sketched, all flat planes and daggers. Every mesa's cluster was tuned to emphasize the highest, central plateau, which met the Wall. Here the buildings resembled crystals of chrysolite and spar, featureless at this distance, divided by walls of deep jade green. The train worked steadily over and between the mesas, rising slowly, crossing trestles when valleys intervened, surrounded by walled throughways on the tablelands. It was an armored, protected millipede crawling laboriously to meet the cloud-worshipped Wall.

Kiril was too dazed to be impressed. The scene rolled by with a featureless, chaotic irregularity. It was meaningless because it was unlike anything he'd ever seen before. Later, perhaps, he might have nightmares about it, but now he could not assimilate. He could only stiffly wait.

Barthel saw nothing but an empty seat on the opposite side of the car. His lips worked.

The highest plateau was breached. The millipede slowed and chuffed, then coasted smoothly into a ceramic-lined tunnel. Daylight flashed as it left the tunnel and slid against a slant-walled building.

They were taken from the car. The entourage of guards and officers in the car surrounded the three foreigners and two nonhumans as if they were some treasure to be protected.

Again, in the interior of the dull, gold ziggurat, they were fed into a cell more spacious and comfortable, but still with the door locked and the walls padded. They were not searched. They'd been closely watched.

Barthel, however, had kept himself immobile throughout the journey. He had been ignored for long moments. No one noticed his hand reaching down to break off a strip of metal edging the seat. Not even Bar-Woten saw.

Only the woman in the seat opposite. She smiled.

Twenty-three

Hours passed in the darkened cell. Kiril, Bar-Woten and Barthel lay on their cots, waiting. Kiril heard Bar-Woten snore. He squeezed his eyes shut, taking refuge in the even deeper darkness. He tried to remember Mediweva. Somehow, he found his way there, and his body relaxed.

Barthel was wide awake. He reached under his shirt and felt for the sharp strip he had pried loose on the train.

His mother moved in the dark, glowing, her true mouth and the mouth in her throat urging him on silently. He hardly understood who or what he was any more. All his world had been shattered, and yet he felt stupid that he had been surprised. The Bey — the Ibisian who had been his master for all his adult life — was after all a murderer and a pillager of Khem, his homeland.

Bar-Woten had said startling things under the influence of the demon's needles. Fifteen years of travel together had not revealed such things. Bar-Woten's drugged ramblings had raised the past to hideous life, bringing back the phantom of his mother — long lost in his thoughts, part of a warm, frightening blankness — haunting Barthel with all the memories and suspicions he had always known would be best left forgotten, dropped like plum stones in a pond.

Bar-Woten stirred in the dark and murmured.

You are no longer Barthel, servant to the Ibisian who killed me, the ghost told her son. *You are Amma bin Akka, and you are free. Prove you are free.*

Barthel stood over the Bey, the Ibisian. He lifted the sharp strip, tears filling his eyes and streaming down his cheeks. He thought, *I have served you, worshipped you, followed you across land and sea. I have loved you. Why must I be the one to kill you?*

He beseeched the ghost, but she would not relent.

You belong with us, she said. *Your sisters are with us. We kept them from the conqueror's hands, as we would have kept you. All of our family, together.* Carried in the Bey's strong arms, rushed from a house full of corpses, Barthel had caught a glimpse of his sisters, their throats cut, lying on their pallet in the two-room mastaba-house, blood dark red in the dusty sunlight from the smoke-hole in the straw roof. Barthel had been little more than a baby; the drugs had opened his earliest memories now, and they were eating him alive. Before the Bey had come to pick him up, he had heard his sisters' shrieks, his father's prayers to Allah, his mother's weeping. Had seen the dull flash of the sheep-knife lifted above the mud-brick partition.

With a strangled shout, Barthel drove the makeshift blade down toward the Ibisian.

Kiril heard a shout and the tearing of fabric. He sat up half awake and grunted a question.

Bar-Woten felt the resistance of flesh and the warmth of spilling blood but by then it was too late. He had reacted with the automatism of a scorpion's tail, had rolled from the point's arc and, not thinking who might be attacking, had thrown up the bedclothes, entangling the assailant. Drops of moisture — Barthel's tears — stung against his cheek. The shadow struck again and again, shrieking and kicking like an enraged child. Knowing with twenty years of combat experience where the weapon was, even in the dark, Bar-Woten grabbed the hand and turned the point inward, driving it home with a kick of his foot against the shattered

184

wrist. The attacker had no chance and perhaps he had known that. With a quiet gasp he went down and whether there had been blood first, or the resistance of the flesh, the snap of bone or the tearing of cloth, there was no knowing. For Bar-Woten, still half-asleep, it was all muddled.

A light came on. Two guards stood sleepy-eyed in the cell's open doorway.

Bar-Woten looked down on his servant from where he lay on the cot. Barthel, tangled in bed-clothes, writhed on the floor, saliva and tears shining on his face and chin. He stared at Bar-Woten.

"Bey!" he said, his voice like a lamb's bleat. Bar-Woten got down on his knees beside the boy and hugged him, his one good eye still dry, but closed.

"They would have killed you," he whispered in Ibisian. Barthel had pulled the point from his stomach and was trying ineffectually to shove it through the Ibisian's thick sailor's coat. Bar-Woten did not block the stabs; they didn't even draw blood. "I was mad from the carnage, and they were slaughtering infants. I could not stand by. I did not know they were your parents."

The guards raised their rifles.

"No!" Kiril shouted. He leaped from his cot and stood before the two. Bar-Woten glanced up at his back, face impassive and white in the sudden glare.

One guard stepped forward and knocked Kiril aside, reaching down to remove the strip of metal from Barthel's grasp. He raised the butt of his rifle to drive back Bar-Woten, but the thin cloaked shadow of the demon hissed in the doorway. The guard stepped aside abruptly, as if stung, bloody point held up as evidence and excuse.

"You should never have left home, Bey," Barthel said, his voice soft and quiet.

"Your pilgrim is still alive, Guest Excellency," the guard said, pointing to Kiril. "By our quick action."

Barthel's face wrinkled in final pain and all the remaining tension left his body. Bar-Woten did not move until the guards pried the corpse from his arms.

Twenty-four

Two of the thin, cloaked demons walked behind Kiril and Bar-Woten. On all sides, armed guards formed walls as the procession moved through a high-walled canyon of steel, glass and concrete. Hundreds of thousands of people watched from tiers of seats on each side of the boulevard. Paper streamers sizzled through the air and confetti fell in thick clouds, getting into their clothes, itching. Kiril vaguely heard the carnival cheers and the cries of "Pilgrim! Pilgrim! Find your way!"

Amplifiers mounted on light standards along the boulevard echoed a tinny refrain:

> "Find your own way, make love to the Wall,
> Be the clown who will learn,
> The fool who might return . . . "

Kiril couldn't make out the rest. It was a mummer's farce, and he was the central caricature, an unspectacular man accompanied by a silent soldier, both of them having come tens of thousands of kilometers to be paraded up this street of the sophisticated English-speakers, met with ridicule and ceremony, sent to the Wall like belled goats.

The demons were taking no chances. Both Bar-Woten and Kiril were accompanying them to the Wall. Kiril was the likely candidate, but who could completely riddle fairy tales, especially those of another species?

Kiril hated them all fiercely. He saw in the English-speakers all the concentrated disease and decay of the Second-born, their science and knowledge contributing little or nothing to remedy their lack of dignity and respect for their fellows.

Kiril hated himself, as well. He had survived. But the incomprehensible violence that had ended Barthel's journey hung like a dead weight around his shoulders. He fell behind Bar-Woten and the guards pushed him on.

The third demon was staying behind as part of an agreement with the English-speakers. The two accompanying them would climb the eight kilometer slope of the Wall with the pilgrim, whichever he might be.

The boulevard ended at the Wall. Kiril and Bar-Woten were given packs of food and climbing equipment. The demons were equipped with steel cylinders and cloth-wrapped parcels. The noise of the crowd subsided behind them.

"This is not by our design, human," one of the demons told Kiril as they started to climb. "We have a journey, also. We all reach our destinations."

Kiril nodded, not facing the silvery mask. A thousand pilgrims had climbed the wall before them, the English-speaker's history books said. The last had been a year ago, before the arrival of the thin ones in their rocket. A fool's parade.

"Why don't they just kill pilgrims and be done with it?" he asked the demon.

"They do not dare. Some pilgrims come from among their own people; they cannot deny the Wall or those who come to it. And sometimes, their pilgrims return."

"Return?"

The demon was silent for a moment. The second demon

stopped climbing and pointed its blank silvery mask at Kiril. A thin whining sound came from under the cloak.

"There have been no pilgrims from this land for ten years," the first continued. "The migrations began only twenty years ago. But we have learned. At other places and along other points of the wall, the streams of pilgrims have increased a thousand-fold. Some cities have been inundated since the fall of the Spire. They are all driven by one thing, that which we drew from your own memory — the loss of a mate. There have been females as well as males."

"Why?"

The enigmatic mask was silent again.

"Don't you know?"

"We do not know," the second demon admitted. "They migrate to appease — " again the whine — "a fairy tale. Most die on the journey. Most are already dust or mud. You have survived."

"I've had help," Kiril said, glancing at Bar-Woten. The Ibisian climbed steadily, silently beside him. "I owe my life many times over to him."

Eight kilometers up the Wall, the English-speakers had told them, a line of circular entrances awaited. The entrances had been surveyed many times in the past; separated by two kilometers, each consisted of a hole ten meters across and fifty meters deep, ending at a blank barrier. If Kiril or Bar-Woten were worthy, the barrier would open. If not, they would probably die trying to descend the slope, too demoralized to be cautious. Either way, the English-speakers would never see them alive again.

Clouds bathed them in cold, neutral wafts of moisture.

As they climbed, Kiril learned from the demons that Obelisks were falling every thirty thousand kilometers, with enormous destruction of landscape and life, the nearest being the Obelisk in Weggismarche. Those who returned to the

189

ravaged land were now able to view most of the Obelisk texts. Soon, most of the inhabitants of Hegira would know — or be forced to know — the history and accomplishments of the First-born.

They would have to accept the truth of what they were — whatever that might be.

Bar-Woten listened. At one point, he stripped away his black patch and cast it down the slope. The sunken, wrinkled pit of his second eye cast the rest of his face out of proportion, giving him a calm, yet leering aspect. The man's silence frightened Kiril more than the demons. *What is he thinking? What actually happened to Barthel?*

Kiril tried to concentrate on the climb, on his aching thighs and calves and arms, on his neck stiff from the cold and from peering ahead, up the slope of the Wall. *This is the last crawl of the migrating worm*, he thought. God's gaze was not intense light, as he had been told by the Franciscans, but cold dank clouds and tears.

For the Wall wept. Its condensation ran in tiny rivulets to the land, gathering to form rivers. The water made the footing slippery, as if they walked up a slope of wet glass — but there was always the traction of the engraved words.

The thin ones climbed steadily, tirelessly, with a wobbling gait, arms reaching out to steady themselves, their cloaked and wrapped bird-legs pumping.

"Why did you come here?" Kiril asked once as they rested. Bar-Woten, two meters higher up the slope, inclined his head to hear their answer.

"We are not sure you can understand," one replied. "We wished to know what happened to us. Long ago, all was bliss and paradise, and we grew. We were all part of — " It whined sharply — "a *reach*. A peak of achievement and understanding. Then, it was all lost, and we had to start

190

from the beginning, in the pain and disaster of youth. It is not precisely the same with you."

"But not so different," Kiril said.

"Perhaps."

"Are the English-speakers going to help you try another way back, if you can't pass through the barrier?" he asked. He motioned to the fog-hidden city below.

"We exchanged knowledge."

That didn't answer his question, but he hadn't really expected an answer. "You don't know what they'll do with your knowledge."

"Yes, we do," one cloaked figure hissed. Bar-Woten glanced at Kiril, but still kept his counsel.

Four kilometers. He hooked his sleeping pouch onto the words with a net of tiny grapples. The thin ones had their own apparatus, slinging themselves in wide straps connected to similar grapples. They replenished something in their suits from the steel cylinders.

Kiril did not sleep well.

With green morning, they fought they way through clouds thick as ghostly foliage. Five kilometers. Six.

"There is the entrance," the figure in black said. They automatically increased their pace, though Kiril was exhausted. Bar-Woten again led the way, silent as ever.

They rested at seven kilometers. The clouds drew together above them and obscured the hole again.

The next day, they stood on the lip of the entrance and stared down the shadowy length of the hole in the Wall.

"There is no barrier," a demon said, hissing faintly behind the words.

The tunnel led deep into the Wall, dark for the first hundred yards, then filled with a dry, faint gray luminosity.

"You have made it, Pilgrim," the other demon said.

Kiril and Bar-Woten tossed aside their climbing tools.

Kiril squatted near the edge to examine the tunnel more closely.

"Do you think I could go in?" Bar-Woten asked. It was the first thing he had said since they began their climb; his voice was soft and low. He leaned over to rub the tunnel's surface with his left palm.

"I don't know," Kiril said. "I hope so. We've all come a long way."

Bar-Woten nodded.

"We would like you to proceed," a demon said behind them. "We will follow."

Kiril got to his feet, slinging the almost-empty pack over his shoulder. There was very little food left; the English-speakers had not been generous. Glancing at Bar-Woten, he began walking down the tunnel. Bar-Woten followed, and behind him, the two thin ones.

Kiril kept his eyes forward. After ten minutes, no barrier presented itself. He looked over his shoulder and saw the Ibisian, and at least fifty yards behind him, the demons, who seemed to be moving through gelatin. The tunnel's entrance was a distant point of white. Bar-Woten nodded at him, smiling faint encouragement. Kiril looked ahead again, then back, and stopped, his breath taking a hitch.

A few yards behind Bar-Woten, the tunnel had sealed itself. The thin ones were nowhere to be seen. "We're alone," he said.

Bar-Woten shivered slightly. "Do we qualify?"

Kiril shook his head slowly. "I don't know any more about this than you do."

"You don't feel anything?"

Kiril sighed. "Nothing."

The Ibisian lifted his arm and pointed down the length of the tunnel. "All we can do is walk, then."

They walked for hours, then paused to rest and eat, and

Kiril lay down in a half-curl to sleep. Bar-Woten sat beside him, knees drawn up under his resting elbows, flicking a strip of cloth from one hand, then drawing it up and rolling it, flicking it again, drawing and rolling . . .

Kiril awakened and watched him. "What do you think we'll find?"

"The Land Where Night Is a River," Bar-Woten said without hesitation.

"But what *is* that?"

"I'm not sure I care any more," the Ibisian said.

Kiril turned away, shaking his head. "He tried to kill you. Why?"

"When the English-speakers drugged us for the demons to listen . . . I think I spoke of Khem, and he must have remembered. He saw very little."

"What happened?"

"It isn't important," Bar-Woten said.

"He was like your son."

Bar-Woten gave Kiril a glance of both agony and barely-contained rage. His lips drew tight and his one eye glittered with tears. The sunken caul of his other eye was also wet. Then the rage seemed to evaporate.

Kiril watched the Ibisian silently crying, both appalled and fascinated. "He deserved to be here with us," he said after a while. "But millions have died already. Whichever god made this happen is a careless god."

Bar-Woten stood abruptly and walked past Kiril down the tunnel.

"Right," Kiril said.

Before the next sleep, they walked ten or eleven kilometers — or as much as fifteen. There was no accurate way of telling distance or time. Still the tunnel was featureless. Kiril felt a touch of fear and the walls seemed to shrink around him. He paused, dizzy and nauseated, and lowered his head. "Wait," he said. Bar-Woten turned to look at his companion.

The tunnel was empty.

Kiril kneeled until he had recovered, and then got to his feet. Bar-Woten was gone. Thinking the Ibisian had gone far ahead of him, Kiril began to run, calling out his name, but the tunnel ended abruptly only a few hundred meters ahead.

He paced back and forth before the blank barrier, not daring to touch it, afraid this was truly the end and he had been rejected, murmuring automatic prayers, but no longer certain to which god if any they were directed. He thought perhaps the Ibisian had been allowed to pass, and his face flushed with anger and a kind of envy. Finally, furious, he reached out to strike the barrier with his fist. His hand vanished and he stumbled through.

At that moment, Kiril began to understand the power of Hegira. Beyond the insubstantial partition was a clear view of darkness and fire doves. He stood in a transparent hemisphere about ten meters across, the glass or whatever substance it was made of supported by a waist-high wall. The air in the chamber was musty but breathable. There was no sign of Bar-Woten.

He walked to the edge, and realized he must be looking over the top of the Wall at the end of the world. The upper surface of the Wall was a featureless dark plain that stretched in front and to each side to a seemingly flat horizon.

Kiril circled to the opposite side of the dome, around the man-high half-circle through which he had entered, and which must have been a kind of doorway. From that vantage, he looked down through a bluish haze and thick layers of clouds to the surface of his world. Holding up a finger, he wonderingly traced rivers and mountain ranges and the broad delta of the Pale Seas. He could make out the cloud-wrapped line of the fallen Obelisk in Weggismarche and Pallasta, and the upright Obelisks of other lands, thousand of kilometers distant.

He slumped to his knees and lifted his elbows to the edge of the dome, leaning his head in the crook of one arm, too astonished to think, much less worry about what had happened to Bar-Woten. For an hour, he stared at the umbers and greens and grays of continents and the blues and more pronounced greens of oceans; russet, sienna and ochre deserts and grassy plains, tracks of mountains spreading like frost on glass, anvils and fish-skeletons of clouds, puffs of storms and whorls of hurricanes, all stretching to a broad line of blue on the high, immensely broad horizon. And rising over land, sea and sky, the stolid needles with their tops of sheet sunlight, on a level with the Wall and the dome. *I am as tall as an Obelisk.*

Then the Obelisks' light faded. The land became shadowy and night snugged fit across Hegira. The fire doves gleamed more brightly without daylight's competition from below.

With a contentment he hadn't known since childhood — a recognition of forces higher than himself, in which he must place his trust or simply give up in despair — he put his gear on the floor of the dome and went to sleep beneath the glimmer of the fire doves.

Bar-Woten found his own barrier. He reached out to feel the plug on the tunnel, and when his hand passed through, he closed his eye and stepped forward resolutely, more than half expecting to die.

Kiril awoke from some vague dream and rolled over on his back.

"Good morning," greeted the man standing over him.

For a moment, with Kiril's vision unfocused, he thought

it might be Bar-Woten, but then he tensed and slowly backed up against the hemisphere's waist-high wall. The man carried a pack, and wore clothes similar to his own, but he was not the Ibisian. His face was well-tanned and deeply grooved with sun-and-wind wrinkles. His hair was a backward-swept mop of solid gray. His nose was an oft-broken, crooked ruin, and he had a grin as devious as his nose, but he did not seem unfriendly. In one hand he clutched a round black ball the size of a small apple. Kiril glanced down at his feet and saw the man wore no shoes.

"You've only been here a little while," the man said. "Need some guidance?" He was speaking Pallastan, not radically different from Teutan, but with an odd inflection.

"I'm sure I do," Kiril said. "How long have you been here?"

"In the observatory? Just a few minutes. You surprised me, lying here. I've been in the Wall for a year, maybe two. I'm not clear about time any more. You're not from Weggismarche, but you speak the tongue fairly well . . . Have you traveled far?"

Kiril got to his feet. "From a place called Mediweva. Thousands of kilometers. Tens of thousands."

The man nodded. "I've heard of it. Sailors bring back stories. Or at least, they used to. Is my country still there? Pallasta?"

Kiril hesitated, then shook his head. "It's in very sad shape."

The man's shoulders slumped. "Then this is my home. My name is Jury." He offered his hand.

"Kiril." The man's grip was firm but not brusque.

"This place will take getting used to. It has a secret, you know. Have you found the secret yet?"

"No, I don't think so," Kiril said. He pointed to the man's clenched hand. "Is it the ball?"

"No," the ball replied in a child's voice. Kiril started back, then caught himself and covered his surprise by reaching down to pick up his pack. The Pallastan smiled.

"Not strictly *the* secret, but it will help you understand. I don't listen to it much any more. You have to ask it a question, and then it will answer, except when you first get yours. Then it tells you what it is."

"We all get one?"

"I assume so. You know about the migration?"

Kiril nodded. "What *is* the ball?"

Jury hefted the object in question and scowled at it. "It says it's part of the world. I don't trust it completely, not now. I keep it around because it knows a few useful things."

"Where do I find mine?"

Jury pointed at the half-circle gate. "Back through there. There's a place where we get food and water, and a place to sleep, if you wish to use it."

"It doesn't go back to the tunnel?"

Jury smiled with some superiority. "You can't get back to the tunnel, and you can't get home again . . . unless you do what it tells you. I haven't. Others have. I don't know where they went. Maybe the ball lies."

Kiril took a deep breath. "Let's go, then."

"Did your woman die, too?" Jury asked as they walked to the other side of the gateway.

"She didn't die. She turned solid, like ice or silver."

"As good as dead. Mine did the same. I listened to legends. My father told me the legends, and what to do. He died of old age just before I left for the Wall. I felt obligated to follow through. Everybody thought I should. But now that I'm here . . . well, it's another story."

"I have some pretty strong reasons," Kiril said. "Show me the way."

Jury stepped forward, but did not enter the gateway.

197

"You came a long way. Saw a lot of strange things, too, I bet."

"Yes."

Jury stepped through first, and Kiril followed.

They stood in a hall, about twice as long as it was wide, and three meters from floor to ceiling. At the end of the hall was a large circular room with an opaque domed ceiling. A glowing bulge at the top of the dome provided heat and light. As he walked around the room, Kiril discovered that parts of the floor were spongy. "You can sleep here," Jury explained.

At the center of the room was an austere white table. As they stepped near, the table hummed and bowls appeared. Two contained a thin, souplike fluid that steamed and gave off an appetizing odor. Others held fruit and raw vegetables. "Thank you," Jury said to the walls. "Always pays to be polite. Of course, they never answer back. Maybe I've been here too long." Jury threw Kiril an appraising glance, then picked up a cup of cool red liquid and toasted Kiril. He squatted on his haunches by the table to eat. Kiril stood nearby, unsure what he was supposed to do.

Jury moved an upside-down bowl on the table, revealing another ball. This one was the color of pewter. "Must be yours," he said, rolling it across the surface at Kiril. Kiril reached out to grab it.

"Well, go ahead, ask it something," Jury encouraged.

Kiril dropped it into his pants pocket. "I'll wait until later."

Jury shrugged and dipped his fingers into the soup, licking them enthusiastically. "No utensils. Make you eat like an animal."

When they had eaten their fill, they moved back from the table and lay down on two spongy areas in the floor. The empty bowls silently vanished, sinking into the table top.

"There's another place you'll want to see before you go to sleep," Jury said. "After a while, you'll get used to the routine. You use the same door, but go to a different place each time. First there's the observatory, where we just were, then here, then the next place." He dropped a fruit core onto the floor. It liquefied and was absorbed. "But never back to the tunnel. Never home. Won't let you . . . unless."

"I'm ready," Kiril said, standing and wiping his hands on his pants. Jury jumped to his feet with a grin and walked back down the hall to the half-circle, and through. Kiril followed.

Why did you come here?

Bar-Woten spun through darkness in a kind of dream, and decided he would not answer questions from somebody or something he could not see.

You are not marked. Why did you come here?

The answers were taken from him anyway, as hard as he fought to close his mind. Then they were presented to him, brushed and groomed — put in order. He listened to this more organized version of his inner voice with little recognition at first.

"I must know what I am, why we are here. I must know why it was necessary for me to kill so many, if the First-born had once been like gods. Why does it all come back to me?"

You accompanied a true pilgrim, one who was marked. Did you protect him?

"Yes. I brought him here, I told him why he must come here. He would not have come without me."

I am grateful for this.

Bar-Woten realized the "I" referred to was Hegira itself, but he was past wonder now.

You were not marked, and are not part of this plan. Still, you have served me. You carried the legend to the pilgrim. Perhaps I in turn can serve you. Where do you wish to go?

"Can you tell me, why all this suffering? Why the fall back to what the First-born were in their youth?"

You may learn that soon enough, from other pilgrims. Where do you wish to go?

"Someplace where I might learn." Bar-Woten compared himself with Kiril, strong and bold soldier and adventurer with reluctant, mystically inclined scholar, and felt an intense envy. Things were all out of proportion. He had been the leader and the instigator. Why had *he* not been marked?

Hegira itself touched his thoughts lightly and found another wish he had hardly acknowledged over the decades. *This much is granted to you*, his world told him, and the darkness began to clear.

Kiril and Jury entered a glass-walled, cramped cabin suspended high above the Wall. From here, to their left they had a direct view of the lands beneath the Wall, and of the rim of the world they had known as their own. Looking down to the right, they saw the outer edge of the Wall. At five thousand kilometer intervals along the Wall's inner edge, overlooking the lands and seas, Kiril discerned the much shorter glowing columns that carried on the light-spreading function of the Obelisks.

Beyond the sinuous, broadly scalloped outer edge, Kiril looked down . . . and down, into a river of endless night. The immense gulf of black meandered between the grayness of the near Wall and yet another Wall beyond, two distinct segments of the world. The two walls and the gulf spanned at least several thousand kilometers, vanishing to either side in very gradual curves. Kiril recalled Bar-Woten's estimate of Hegira's size — 249,000 kilometers in diameter — and did a quick calculation. Hegira had a circumference of about 780,000 kilometers.

Beyond the river of night, contained within the next Wall, was yet another land. It seemed different, as if seen through a distorted red glass. That, Kiril guessed, was the home of the demons — the thin ones.

He shook his head, dizzy. "Where are we?" he asked, feeling sudden vertigo.

"No need to worry," Jury assured him. "If you look down on the other side, you'll see we're on top of a tall, thin tower. It holds us up here. We're not flying or falling."

"What's that beyond the river, the gap?"

"Another part of Hegira. Ask the ball. It'll tell you more, but you might not understand. It has difficulty speaking to mere humans, mere Second-born."

"How much will I understand?"

"That depends on how much you learned before you got here. If you're one of those crazy English-speakers, you might understand a lot. If you're like me, you might spend months listening, trying to understand, and get only a little. I was just a road-crew worker."

The next section of Hegira moved perceptibly, spinning opposite the section containing the land where he had been born, where he had lived and traveled. He removed the ball from his pocket. "What's in the gap?" he asked it.

"Please specify," the ball requested in a slightly different, but still childlike voice.

"What's in the darkness between the Walls?"

"Emptiness; a near vacuum. At the center of Hegira, beneath the counter-rotating segments, there is a singularity."

"Ah," Jury said. "That's a hard one. It'll take a while to explain that one."

"Then I'll ask later."

"Just as hard later."

"What is Hegira?" Kiril asked the ball.

"I'll answer that," Jury interrupted.

"Misinformation is not allowed," both balls said together. "This extension will answer," Kiril's ball continued singly.

"I can tell him in words he'll understand!" Jury protested.

"You do not understand yourself, yet," his ball warned. "And there can be no brief explanation."

"Let's put these things down for a minute," Jury said, exasperated. He reached for Kiril's ball but Kiril withdrew it, clutching it to his chest.

"Stop it," he demanded. "I'm getting confused and angry."

"Jury has not made a crossing," the balls said in unison. "There can be no understanding without a crossing."

"It's lying," Jury said with a sneer on his already crooked lips.

"Is my woman's doppelganger on the other side?" Kiril asked.

"Yes."

"Your woman has no double out there, nor does mine," Jury said.

"Incorrect."

"Put that thing down and come listen!" The Pallastan beseeched with both hands, the left trying to muffle his own sphere.

"I'm sorry. I'll stick with the ball," Kiril said. He felt some of Bar-Woten's instincts guiding him, wherever the Ibisian was now.

"I have no reason to cross," the Pallastan said wearily, sighing. "The Obelisk wiped out my country. My woman has to be dead."

"Did you ask whether she's alive?"

"No. I don't want to know. All right, you're so curious,

do as you please. Ask it everything. You'll end up like the others who have passed through here — you'll never be seen again!" Jury's face was a mask of forced mirth, eyes wide. His hands trembled. He exited through the gateway and Kiril was alone.

He looked down at the ball, no larger than an apple, and tried to gather his questions in order of importance. "Tell me what Hegira is," he demanded again.

"This question will take a long time to answer. It requires a history of the First-born."

"I'm ready," Kiril said.

"It will not be told in mere words," the ball warned. "There is not time."

Kiril nodded. "Go ahead."

Bar-Woten shook himself awake. His clothes were wet with dew and muddy; he was surrounded by rough clods of dirt. Above, the night's last few fire doves hung like tiny lanterns in the sky. The soldier's anger was slow in coming; he had to remember where he had been, and what he had been told, and then he had to decide it was not all a dream. At first, he got to his feet and looked around the newly-ploughed field for Barthel and Kiril. When the memory of Barthel's death returned to him, it was too painful and immediate to be a delusion; Bar-Woten cursed and kicked at clods. It had all been real: the decades-long March, the journey, the capture, the death, the separation in the tunnel — and his denial by Hegira.

"God damn you!" he shouted, stomping clods. "God damn you!"

Then his discipline reasserted itself, and he straightened out of his discouraged slouch. Where was he?

There was the field, and low hills around it. The smell of

a moderate-sized body of water, faintly scented by lilies. It was all familiar . . .

Dawn came in a rush to the land, the sky passing through its spectrum and sheets of light growing between the Obelisks. That much he knew, if not where he was . . .

With the dawn, a flock of large birds rose in a pale mass from beyond the hills. He heard a farmer's coarse voice singing and the lowing of cattle . . . The farmer was singing in Ibisian.

The birds were ibises. They flew overhead, swooping low, welcoming him. Bar-Woten stared up, blinking in wonder.

After twenty years, he was home.

There was no immediate revelation of mystical completeness and beauty, only a child's voice informing him this was business for cerebral absorption and not religious inspiration. Generations after could look back upon the story (as Kiril would tell it; he saw himself surrounded by legions of children, stretching off on all sides) with awe if they wished, but for now it had to be explicated coldly and rationally.

No human mind had put the story together. Kiril detected a weariness in Hegira's voice, not physical or even spiritual, rather a fatigue that plagued the very medium through which it thought. The effect was that of falling dust and enclosing darkness, of a job approaching completion, with only a few thousand more years to go.

Kiril began to tremble. Pictures came to his mind rapidly, faster than he could consciously see them; sounds, smells, histories, overviews, impressions, even personalities of cultures and individuals.

He understood very little. Some of it was hideously alien to him. But he listened anyway.

Twenty-five

I have built this world called Flight, have designed it and arranged for its construction, have populated it with beings of all kinds, and have started again the process of action and event, that these beings might exist and think as did living things long ago.

The time comes for all the beings on Hegira to know why they are called Second-born. You are no less than the First-born, but serve a different purpose. You are descendants and seed, and your life is the agony of an egg . . .

Kiril sat on the floor of the cramped cabin, high above his world, and squeezed his head to quell a headache. He stood and stretched his muscles, exhausted. Jury had been correct; he understood very little. He felt close to bursting, but his conscious awareness had not integrated all the visions and data he now contained; it would take years for him to do so, if he ever managed.

What is Hegira? he asked himself.

Hegira is a hollow shell made up of sections like latitudinal slices of an empty fruit rind. At its center is a singularity, an extremely compressed sphere of matter so dense that virtually nothing can escape from the well of its gravitation. This singularity, or black hole, or frozen star, or superpoint mass, spins. When the inner surfaces of Hegira's sections pare off bits of themselves, and shoot these pieces around the singularity, they return with even greater energy, withdrawn from the spin. This process powers the world. Think of an enormous top that spins only on the inside.

He stared across the daylight surfaces of the two sections, and then into the blackness between, and with an inner eye saw these things happening, felt the world's pulse and progress, and its age.

The fire doves are other worlds like Hegira, some larger, many smaller, containing many different kinds of life-forms.

In a few thousand years, it would all stop; the singularities of all the worlds would be tapped out. The worlds would become cold and dead.

Before that time, he and all the pilgrims would have to tell the stories not contained on the Obelisks, to push their peoples into leaving Hegira and migrating outward.

"Oh, Lord," he moaned. Some of what he felt within was blasphemous. Some of the things he saw could sear the souls of those who were not prepared. His job would be hideously difficult.

All the worlds like Hegira together create a singularity with themselves inside, a larger, less dense and more diffuse mass, a kind of bubble with its own separate existence. This universe-in-itself floats through the destruction of the First-born's old universe, already dying or dead. A new universe is forming around this egg, and even now the egg begins to crack, its rents and distortions revealing the new universe. You have seen these as the nights with stars . . .

"They'll kill me if I preach these things," Kiril said. He thought of Mediweva and its citizens, of all they did not know, and cringed.

When these distortions occur, we take our bearings in the new universe, and decide what you will have to face. The new universe is not exactly like the old.

Bar-Woten had intuited as much, months past.

That succeeding universes differ was known long before the

Unknown Span. To adapt to these conditions, you are not precisely like the First-born. The small differences these changes have made in the preparation of the worlds are reflected in the anomalies of animal and plant life. The Second-born are not precisely like the First-born. They are much smaller . . .

Kiril stood and passed through the door, frightened, almost panicked by what he felt within. But he did not return to the living quarters. The tower cabin vanished, and he found himself facing another long tunnel. He glanced back at the doorway, and was reminded of the spirit-blocking slabs in Golumbine. "Where am I?" he asked the ball clutched in his hand.

"If you walk to the end of this tunnel, you will cross the gulf between sections and come to the other Wall."

"Why do I have to go there? What will I find there?"

"That is where you'll find your double."

Kiril paused. "Why there? Why not here?"

The ball did not answer. *That's the way it is, that's all,* he answered for himself. "What if that isn't good enough? What if I don't cross?"

"Then you will remain here like Jury. You have come too far to stop now."

Kiril looked down the length of the tunnel. Every ten paces, a protruding black band marked the circumference, and a raised red pathway showed him where to walk. *Red carpet.* It seemed to stretch to infinity. Behind him, it stretched as far, interrupted only by the doorway.

"You explained all this to Jury, too."

"It is best not to hesitate," the child's voice warned.

"My woman is alive on the other side?"

"In a manner of speaking."

That wasn't as definite as he would have wished. He hesitated. But unlike Jury, he had to act for at least two others: for Barthel, who was dead, and for Bar-Woten, wherever he was. And he had to finish his quest to find Elena, though he could hardly remember what she had looked like. Nevertheless, she was a steady, painful memory, and any chance to be rid of that pain, of all his past obligations, was more than welcome.

Still, perversely, he hesitated. He asked the ball more questions: why, on Hegira, a woman could only bear two children before becoming infertile; how long the Second-born had lived on Hegira; why all Second-born children were able to read Obelisk script from birth, but did not necessarily understand the languages; what part animals played on Hegira; and so on.

The ball answered in its weary child's voice whenever the answer could be briefly given. Kiril still found things confusing. These matters of universes and singularities were clearly beyond him, though no doubt they would be discussed on the Obelisks.

Now that he had some of the answers he had been looking for, he could not completely accept them. All of the life and humanity and history he was familiar with had to be more than a single egg shot with thousands of others into a dead eternity, a diaspora of silkseed worlds.

Kiril took a deep breath and began walking down the tunnel. "All right," he said. "I'll take it on faith, for now." Under his breath, he added, "But if this is all a fantastic lie . . . "

The journey took only a few moments. After several dozen steps, his vision blurred. He rubbed his eyes and saw another doorway blocking the tunnel a few steps ahead. Following the red path, he stepped through.

Twenty-six

Jury lay on the floor before him, asleep. Kiril nearly fell over him. The Pallastan sat up quickly. "Careful, there!" he said. He stood and brushed himself down fastidiously.

"I thought you weren't going to cross," Kiril said, staring in wonder at what lay around them.

"You shamed me into it," Jury said, glancing at him sidewise. "I got sick of sponging off that table back there. Besides, I asked the ball if my woman was alive. It said there was no way she could be killed, in her present condition. It might take me a while to find her, however. In an English-speaker's museum, maybe, or a circus sideshow . . ."

The chamber they stood in was so broad its far edge seemed lost, yet the ceiling was low enough to seem oppressive, only a few centimeters above their heads. The wall of the chamber nearest them, behind the doorway, was divided into coffin-sized partitions, all covered by transparent doors, all apparently empty.

The air was cold and antiseptic-smelling. A thin, rubbery covering on the floor deadened their footsteps.

Kiril removed the ball from his pocket. "What do we do now?" he asked.

"Locate the booth that has a light in it," it answered. "As there are two of you, there will be two booths near each other."

"I don't see any," Jury said, turning around.

"Follow the perimeter until you do."

They set out around the chamber. As they walked, Jury's face wrinkled, as if he was both anxious and reluctant to talk. Finally, his anxiety won out. "You learned everything?" he asked, walking backwards ahead of Kiril.

"I suppose so."

"Did you understand it?"

Kiril shook his head.

"We could talk about it. Compare things. This might take a while. Maybe we could tell whether they've lied to us or not."

That didn't seem a bad idea. They talked.

The First-born worked and loved and suffered to achieve what they achieved, and they did well. The Obelisks tell their story to the end of their existence as physical beings . . .

Your form-ancestors lived on old Earth until they could send ships far out to the planets around their star, called the sun. They populated the planets where possible and sent more advanced ships out to other stars. At first the journeys were slow, but their knowledge increased rapidly, and old laws bowed to new refinements. Ships soon traveled very fast, shooting through the distances between stars in days and weeks and months instead of lifetimes.

"I don't understand what stars are," Jury said, shaking his head. Kiril explained as well as he was able.

There were many other intelligent species besides your form-ancestors. Sometimes they met, and at first the meetings were confused, often destructive, yet always educational. Two thousand years of interaction made your form-ancestors part of a very accomplished interstellar civilization, with the cooperation of thousands of non-human intelligences, many of them the form-ancestors of other beings on Hegira and its companion worlds. This civilization filled the whirlpool of three hundred billion stars that the First-born called their galaxy.

In these times, your form-ancestors changed themselves by

adapting biologically and mechanically to live in places where they would otherwise die. Some grew used to deep space, far from the attractions of planets. Still others, to live in the peculiar places where ships went to travel faster than beams of light, adapted themselves to new sets of spaces and times.

"God help us all," Jury exclaimed. "Nothing could make me understand that." Kiril, however, could clearly see these forms in his head. They were terrifying and beautiful, almost angelic.

Wars and disputes broke out between the different varieties of humanity, and between humans and other beings, and between other beings and different forms of their own kind. It was a cruel, restless age, full of change and growth and pain.

In time, some species found it desirable to mingle their patterns with each other. The results were clumsy at first, and progress difficult, but soon there were as many crossbred beings as there were individuals of distinct species. It was not a sexual communion in the usual sense; rather, it was an exchange of strengths and a repression of weaknesses. All benefited. Your form-ancestors disappeared as a distinct species.

For ages, all the species had been blown about by a wind they had hardly been aware of. They looked back and saw that on their home worlds they had been both muscle and seed, like the pods in a poppy plant. Their intelligence and technology had resulted in a building of muscular tensions, which had exploded to carry them far out into space. Their individual spirits, they learned, had been subservient to a higher force, which they had always thought was more primal — the propagation of living forms.

They discovered a genetic similarity between species, rooted in the nature of matter and energy itself, and they discovered that to reach higher stages of development, most species would have to combine.

It soon became apparent that non-living matter played much the same part in the life-history of the galaxy that calcium in bones and dead hair and skin play in individual biological beings. The inorganic world is actually shaped by the organic for its own needs.

Natural extensions of living things into other spaces and times behaved according to laws as strict as any for the conscious world of the First-born. So-called ghosts, demons and other influences were extensions of their living counterparts and served definite purposes, either as repositories of racial memory or protection from destructive forces — much as your dead outer skin works to keep you from harm. This interaction of states of life and death gave a new clue as to how the First-born must adapt and change. Just as the migration of life from galaxy to galaxy began, the Space Age, which lasted a mere four thousand Earth years, became subservient to another far longer, longer age, the Age of Dissolution.

Description now is far more difficult. Some form-ancestors were shaped much like yourself, even then, thinking in much the same way. There are backwaters in any development, especially when the development is rapid. But other species and super-species were advancing to the point where language using words cannot describe them.

Suffice it to say that organic and inorganic merged throughout thousands of galaxies. For a time, those left in the backwaters thought they lived in a largely dead universe, with only stars and rocky worlds left to explore. They could not see what was actually around them; it would have been easier for a bacterium in a man's gut to understand the man.

Metaphysics became as fluid a tool as physics. Realities were altered and tailored. The Age of Dissolution blended into a new period, the Unknown Span.

To assign lengths of time to the Unknown Span is not appropriate. It would be better to assign energy levels and degrees of equations describing basic entropic functions, which had not,

212

and could not, be altered. The Unknown Span soon approached the death of the super-organism that the universe had always been, and that only now was self-aware. Soon, life would have to spread itself to the universe that would arise from the death of the old.

All things are nested together, and between all things there must be commerce and exchange. In that Unknown Span, Hegira and all its companion worlds were created. Hegira is itself aware and alive.

Jury squatted to rest. The booths were still empty and dark, and they had been walking for five hours. "I am so stupid," he moaned. "What good am I as a pilgrim?"

Kiril didn't answer. The question had occurred to him, as well.

In another hour, when they were about to give up and try to find the doorway again, they found the pair of booths, both filled with an opaque, milky glow. They peered in and saw nothing, but before they could ask the balls another question, sparks and rainbows whittled away at the milkiness within the booths. They then appeared to contain two young men.

One resembled the young scrittori who had fallen and killed himself on Obelisk Tara, in Mediweva, it seemed so long ago: Elena's double. The other was familiar to Jury.

Abruptly, the figures in the booths faded and vanished. Kiril felt a sudden snapping-to within him, an almost nauseating integration that told him more than words their quest was at an end.

"Wait!" Kiril shouted, pounding on the glass. Jury stood limply nearby and tittered, holding two fingers over his mouth like a clown. He broke into raucous laughter.

"Now you can return home," the balls said in unison.

"But we have to take them back with us," Kiril protested hoarsely.

"No need. Both are dead. There can be no returning for them now. All you have to do is return with what you saw here. In fact," and the voices seemed to be speaking through smiles, "your women are already free of their affliction."

"We have to go back now," Jury said matter-of-factly. "My woman will be half out of her mind if she wakes up and finds everything in shambles. I have to be with her. If she hasn't awakened . . . buried alive someplace." His face paled.

"She is alive," the ball reassured him.

"How do we get back?" Kiril asked.

"Find the gate. Enter."

Whether it was the same gate or not, they never knew. They said their farewells rapidly, eager to be done with each other, to try to get back to reality and away from this knowledge-filled madness. They entered the door a few seconds apart and never saw each other again.

Kiril awoke from a sound night's sleep on a hillside in a country he barely recognized, clothed but unshod, and minus his ball and pack. A local sheriff arrested him for vagrancy a day later as he walked along a narrow dirt cart road, and he was taken to a deputato.

It took him three weeks in custody to prove he was who he claimed to be. A visiting church cleric from his village, dough-cheeked and acne-scarred, another student of the Franciscans, was brought in to identify him, and the deputato released Kiril into the hands of his former order. The cleric lent him an ass and together, poor and humble yet somehow happy, they trekked across four hundred kilometers of Mediweva, resting at village inns of varying repute. Nothing seemed to have changed much. The knowledge of the English-speakers had yet to come this far south.

Obelisk Tara was their guide and beacon. After two

weeks of travel, interrupted by visits to the church of local districts — the cleric's business — they came to the village where Kiril had been raised. Here they parted company. Kiril shook the hooded man's travel-roughened hand. "Go with God," he told him.

Then he found the large, ancient stone house of Elena's family, hidden deep in a forest of conifers near the village. The estate was empty but for a plump, tired-looking servant, who greeted him with no enthusiasm whatsoever. "Nobody's here," the servant told him. "They've gone to the wedding."

"What wedding?"

The answer he received was brusque. "The Lady Elena has been restored to health, and is about to marry a fine young man, a prelate of respectable family and sound means."

That, Kiril thought, would not do at all. How would Bar-Woten handle this situation?

"Where will the wedding be?"

At the family ranch in the north, the servant told him reluctantly, butting a broom handle nervously on the floor. This tall, strong-looking and exceedingly ragged young man bothered him — frightened him, if the truth be known. Despite his strange eyes, he almost seemed familiar . . .

"Don't I know you?" the servant asked as Kiril turned to go.

"Yes. We met some time ago, before Elena . . . " He shook his head. No time to waste. "Thank you."

A bank account he had never touched held funds for his scrittori apprenticeship. He was glad now he hadn't turned it over to the Brotherhood of Francis. He proved his identity to an officer of the bank with his signature and a code word that he remembered with some difficulty, his head was so full now of odds and ends. Retrieving these meager funds, he bought passage on a steam wagon.

215

The steam wagon, crowded with farmers and salesmen traveling to the small communities in the highlands, chugged and hissed for hours, climbing steadily if laboriously along the irregular grades. In a small town near the estate, Kiril left the steam wagon and hired a two-passenger steam-cart to take him the rest of the way, and to await his needs.

By early evening, Kiril jumped from the cart near the gate to the ranch and walked unobserved to the steps of the stone house. He stood by a window to the left of the porch, standing on tiptoe atop a split log to peer through thin lace curtains. He could see inside well enough, but the large family room was empty. He frowned fiercely, then lowered his head as a woman passed near the window. Cautiously, he angled his head to one side and lifted an eye above the sill. A group of seven or eight entered the room, talking among themselves.

Kiril recognized a few, among them Lisbeth, Elena's godmother, a slow, dull woman, earthy and direct. She spoke to a man whose back was turned. Her expression was more animated than usual. The man turned; he appeared to be half-asleep. Kiril knew the lassitude one could fall into, listening to Lisbeth.

Behind a young couple nearest the corner desk stood Elena's youngest brother, working string figures on his fingers. He closely resembled the doppelganger whose death had begun Kiril's journey, it seemed an age ago.

Kiril circled around the house, keeping a close lookout for anyone who might see him. He felt like a burglar. Anger was building in him at the thought that a simple church prelate — a godly man, no doubt, pious and inexperienced and kind — might have already sampled what he had gone to the end of the world to save. Kiril's face flushed at the thought. Not even the memory of distant Golumbine could dispel his jealousy; in fact, it stung him to further resolve.

He had given up more than time to reach this goal! He had given up the basic, dumb satisfaction he might have had if he had stayed in Mediweva, contented in his life and work. He had given up all possibility of finding an uncomplicated love and a simple existence among his fellow citizens.

Kiril returned to the front porch and took a deep breath. No more skulking. He would be direct. The sky was already darkening. In an hour or so the fire doves would be out, and if he didn't act before then, he feared the steam cart would leave and strand him until morning. The driver could not expect a handsome tip from this ragged stranger. He had to move quickly.

Kiril knocked heavily on the wooden door. Endless seconds later a thin, small male servant dressed in ceremonial dark green answered. "I'm a friend of the family. I'd like to speak with Elena's father, please, on an important matter."

"The master is busy at the moment," the weary-eyed man answered, staring at him balefully. Kiril was not recognized. "He's eating dinner and entertaining guests. May I announce you?"

The servant behaved as if this were an exceedingly generous offer.

"No," Kiril said, stepping swiftly around the man and marching through the anteroom and hallway. "No time!"

The family had just finished the evening meal. A few guests had sauntered into the outer rooms, but most lounged before a large fire in the tall, wood-paneled sitting room. Elena sat at the knees of a young, actually fairly handsome man Kiril knew immediately was the prelate, her husband-to-be. Kiril stood in the entrance to the sitting room for a breath or two, all eyes turning to examine him. Elena's gaze, most important of all, went wide, and she choked in her cup of wine.

217

"I've come," he said, knowing it was melodramatic, and pausing for even more emphasis. "Come for what is mine."

It was a grand, stomach-churning moment. His tongue was sure but his hands trembled.

"Alfred Karl!" the father shouted at the servant. "Did you let this man into my house unannounced?"

"I let myself in. Elena, come here."

The father and mother then recognized him. "Where have you been?" the father asked, approaching him with squared shoulders and a dour look. Kiril had once had great respect for this man's strength of body as well as character. Now he felt they were at least evenly matched.

"I will not be stopped," he said quietly, holding up a calloused hand. He was sleek and muscular beneath his soiled white clothes, and well-tanned, an altogether different sort compared to the pale, scholarly fellow who had wooed, mourned and then vanished over two years before. "I've gone through hell for you," he said to Elena. She didn't look the same, somehow; less radiant than he had expected. Tired. She had been through quite a strain in the past few weeks, he guessed; the marriage had been hastily arranged, no doubt, after her revival.

"Kiril, I can't leave now," Elena said, her strained, pale face wet with tears. Her obvious confusion pained him deeply. She had not felt the passage of time. Everything was topsy-turvy for her. "Something has happened . . ."

He walked across the room, over the century-old woven rug at the center of the half-circle of chairs, and reached down for her arm. The prelate gaped and puffed and stood up, almost falling back over his chair as his legs flexed abruptly against the frame. "What are you doing?" he demanded. His voice, compared to Kiril's, was a small and undistinguished yap. Still, Kiril acknowledged, trying to be fair, his face did show some courage. He felt sorry for the man.

Kiril grasped Elena's arm as gently as possible. Her wide, green eyes accused him, shocked and — he thought, he hoped — happy for his return. He lifted her from the floor. The prelate swung at him and seemed to magically miss, as if Kiril were a ghost.

"I can't go!" Elena wailed. "You can't take me back! It's all arranged."

"I can, and will," Kiril said softly. "You can make up your mind away from these people." He rushed her into the night, dancing agilely through the arms of servants, parents and the poor prelate. She did not protest once they were outside. The steam cart waited at the end of the road, beyond the gate. Kiril picked her up and set her in the cab, then climbed in after her. The driver moved the cart off at his command. Behind them, a crowd spilled out onto the road, murmuring, shouting. The prelate chased them for perhaps a quarter of a mile, then gave up, collapsing on the gravel.

Elena, stiff as a board, sat in one corner of the cab and stared at him, shocked and frightened. "Come on," Kiril murmured, unable to meet her eyes. "I haven't been gone that long, not as far as you're concerned."

"They said you'd been gone for years while I was asleep."

"You weren't asleep."

"In a coma, then."

"You weren't in a coma."

Elena suddenly went limp, like an unstrung puppet, and sobbed. "Where have you been?" she wailed. She hit his shoulder with several stinging slaps. "Where in God's name have you been?"

"I've traveled a long way," Kiril said. "I have a lot to do here. I'm a determined man now." But he still felt like a

219

young boy in places. His assurance did not run through him unflawed.

The cart stopped abruptly, and the driver swung down from his seat, cursing and loudly praying. The illumination of the night had subtly changed; it was brighter. Kiril helped Elena down from the coach and waved his hand at the stars in the sky, and the wisps of glow in between.

"See all this?" he asked. She nodded, awestruck, but not, he noted with approval, particularly frightened. She would suit him just fine after all, he thought. She was resilient.

"I know what it is," he said. "Most of it, anyway. I'll explain it to you soon." For an hour, they stood beneath the young, strange glow of the new night sky.

Finally, Kiril helped her back into the cab. The driver came back from the woods, where he had abruptly departed, wringing his hands and complaining bitterly. He took his position on the cart and glared at his passengers.

"How soon can you explain?" Elena asked.

"I have to put it all together in my head," Kiril said. "Maybe you can help me."

She regarded him sharply, then reached for his hand. "They said you were gone for good."

Kiril smiled. "You knew better, I hope."

"No," she said, turning away petulantly. "I really didn't."

Kiril's heart leaped. This was the Elena he remembered, difficult but not impossible. As the cart lurched forward, he reached out to draw her to him, and she did not resist . . . much.

Twenty-seven

When the stars came out again, Bar-Woten was spending the night at a small hostel near the city of Frelang. He had been kicked out of three towns already, called a liar and a tramp. Few believed him when he told his story of returning from Sulay's march. Sulay was an ugly legend in Ibis; he had taken most of the country's youth on a journey from which few, if any, had returned. He had depleted the countryside of manpower and wealth.

Discreetly, the far-traveled soldier inquired about returning pilgrims, people who had abruptly appeared, crazy people who proclaimed visions and vast knowledge. He had heard of a few, and he was intent on tracking down at least one. Perhaps these pilgrims had also been on Sulay's march, and had settled down years past — deserters, caught up in the life of another country. Perhaps they had been seduced by thoughts of domesticity, and fate had tricked them, turning their husbands or wives into blocks of merciless silver, sending them on a long quest.

It seemed difficult to believe that anybody else had traveled to the Wall but one of Sulay's soldiers. Still, he supposed, anything was possible.

When he found a pilgrim, he would ask questions. He would protect the pilgrim, from himself or others. He would guide the pilgrim politically and, perhaps, help establish the new order.

Bar-Woten, Bear-killer of the One-eyed God, soldier and

would-be-pilgrim, stood beneath the wispy night with the sounds of drunken revelry coming from a nearby tavern. He felt a familial contempt for his ignorant fellow creatures. Something big was happening, that much was obvious.

He would be a part of it, or he would die trying.

He owed that much to the ghosts of those he had killed. To Barthel. Even, he thought, to Sulay, so despised in his homeland now.

He savored the wildness of the new sky, its apparent strangeness and youth. Here was challenge, opportunity. He had not the slightest idea what it all meant, but he knew one thing.

The stars were here to stay.

And he would find a place in them.

OTHER TITLES AVAILABLE FROM
VGSF

The prices shown below were correct at the time
of going to press (January 1987)

☐	03995 7	WITCH WORLD	*Andre Norton*	£2.50
☐	03990 6	THE MASKS OF TIME	*Robert Silverberg*	£2.95
☐	04008 4	HEGIRA	*Greg Bear*	£2.95
☐	04032 7	THE FACELESS MAN	*Jack Vance*	£2.50
☐	03987 6	NIGHT WALK	*Bob Shaw*	£2.50
☐	04009 2	ANGEL WITH THE SWORD	*C.J. Cherryh*	£2.95
☐	04022 X	MISSION OF GRAVITY	*Hal Clement*	£2.50
☐	03988 4	THE OTHER SIDE OF THE SKY		
			Arthur C. Clarke	£2.95

Available June 1987

☐	03996 5	WEB OF THE WITCH WORLD	*Andre Norton*	£2.50
☐	04010 6	EYE AMONG THE BLIND	*Robert Holdstock*	£2.50

Available July 1987

☐	04007 6	STAR GATE	*Andre Norton*	£2.50
☐	03989 2	TO LIVE AGAIN	*Robert Silverberg*	£2.95

Also available: GOLLANCZ CLASSIC SF

☐	03819 5	THE SIRENS OF TITAN	*Kurt Vonnegut*	£3.50
☐	03821 7	MORE THAN HUMAN	*Theodore Sturgeon*	£2.95
☐	03820 9	A TIME OF CHANGES	*Robert Silverberg*	£2.95
☐	03818 7	NOVA	*Samuel R. Delany*	£2.95
☐	03849 7	THE CITY AND THE STARS	*Arthur C. Clarke*	£2.95
☐	03850 0	THE DOOR INTO SUMMER	*Robert Heinlein*	£2.95
☐	03852 7	WOLFBANE	*Frederik Pohl & C.M. Kornbluth*	£2.95
☐	03851 9	THE REPRODUCTIVE SYSTEM	*John Sladek*	£2.95
☐	03978 7	A FALL OF MOONDUST	*Arthur C. Clarke*	£3.50
☐	03980 9	A WREATH OF STARS	*Bob Shaw*	£2.95
☐	03979 5	ROGUE MOON	*Algis Budrys*	£2.95
☐	03981 7	MAN PLUS	*Frederik Pohl*	£3.50

Available June 1987

☐	03993 0	INVERTED WORLD	*Christopher Priest*	£3.50
☐	04061 0	FLOWERS FOR ALGERNON	*Daniel Keyes*	£2.95

All these books are available at your shop or newsagent or can be
ordered direct from the publisher. Just tick the titles you want and fill
in the form overleaf.

VGSF, Cash Sales Department, PO Box 11, Falmouth, Cornwall.

Please send cheque or postal order, no currency.

Please allow cost of book(s) plus the following for postage and packing:

UK customers – Allow 60p for the first book, 25p for the second book plus 15p for each additional book ordered, to a maximum charge of £1.90.

BFPO – Allow 60p for the first book, 25p for the second book plus 15p per copy for the next seven books, thereafter 9p per book.

Overseas customers including Eire – Allow £1.25 for the first book, 75p for the second book plus 28p for each additional book ordered.

NAME *(Block letters)* ....

ADDRESS...

....

....